IELTS

BEST BOOKS
倍斯特出版事業有限公司
Best Publishing Ltd.

雅思聽力聖經

模擬試題

韋爾 ◎ 著

英式發音 QRCODE
DOWNLOAD

精選四回，**迅速釐清** 學習盲點
修正惱人的「7.5-8.0」瓶頸期躍至 **9.0佳績**

活化思緒、準確定位關鍵考點＋掌握隱晦難答的同義轉換

將初階到進階的**同義表達分拆**並融入模擬試題中，且同步**強化定位**和**理解能力**，觸類旁通應對各類變化題。

跨領域主題迅速擴充知識面

藉由**多元主題**訓練**大腦思路**和**組織能力**，省去鑽研演練龐大題庫的時間，事半功倍獲取9.0高分。

PREFACE 作者序

　　這本聽力模擬試題有別於坊間聽力試題，在 section 2 的部分都改成了原本在 section 3 or 4 才會出現的演講類話題，此舉能大幅提升考題的鑑別度，也能跟所有官方聽力試題有所區別。其中的原因在於，撰寫近幾年的官方試題（例如：劍 10-劍 16）並詳細統計所有閱讀和聽力測驗的答對題數，只是紀錄的撰寫試題當下的實力或部分進步的過程。然而，考生更需要的是較難的練習題和提升整合能力的試題，並期許在演練後迅速獲得實力上的提升，而非海量演練一堆試題，但是聽力分數卻考了數次仍在 7.5 分等等的。因此，具備鑑別度、整合能力和跨主題的試題是必須的。我想這也是考生最關心的，為何有劍橋雅思官方試題，我還需要這本書籍呢？如果已經反覆撰寫數次劍橋雅思官方的聽力和閱讀試題的考生，聽力和閱讀仍停滯在某個分數段，劍橋雅思官方試題顯然已經不能成為欲突破某個分數段或大幅進步的考生的需求了，而僅是檢測當下撰寫試題所反應的水平了。

　　以第 6 個講堂為例，當中就包含了探討三本文學經典作品《*Middlemarch*》、《*The History of Tom Jones, a Founding*》、《*Gone with the Wind*》（多元主題的靈活考題），能迅速提升考生的整合能力。提到整合能力，考生可能會覺得模糊。進一步地說明整合能力的話，就是代表這些試題能提升的一定不只是聽力的單項能力。而是包含「聽力＋口說」或是「聽力＋寫作＋口說」等多方面的規劃。在演練這些試題時，考生其他單項的成績也會有顯著的進步。以這個講堂所探討的婚姻話題為例，（除了是寫聽力試題外）也能看成是在答寫作題目。因為雅思寫作考試不論題目，都不求對錯，而是考生看到題目後是否能言之有物，提出自己的論點並用無文法修辭錯誤的文句表達出來。在這個話題中提到「關於婚姻，父母該提供建議亦或是全然遵照小孩意願呢？」講堂的話題，藉由三本名著探討了正、反兩方的論述，除了與寫作相關外，考生是否也會想到這樣也與「演說和辯論有關」，所以這樣的一個話題是無形中就提升考生「**聽力＋寫作＋口說**」三方面的整合能力。

在《亂世佳人》和《米德爾鎮的春天》，考生可以明顯看到思嘉麗的父親傑拉爾德和多羅西亞的伯父（布魯克），兩人對於女兒擇偶採取了完全不同的方法。傑拉爾德甚至分析了事情的許多面向給女兒聽，認為婚姻大事是要父母作主，他甚至勸女兒不要想要試圖去改變一個男人。而布魯克則認為多羅西亞想嫁誰就嫁吧！他何必因為自己是長輩就扮演智者去評斷這個婚姻是好或壞呢？而書中多羅西亞的另一位追求者詹姆士也有不同的見解，他認為多羅西亞太年輕了根本無法判斷對方是否合適自己（小說後面也證實了他所說的完全沒錯，多羅西亞需要別人提供判斷，她丈夫在婚後總是忽略女人的感受...）。不過，不論長輩們是否給意見，兩位女主角都憑自己的判斷去選擇了自己想要的婚姻，但結果卻都不好。演講結尾也把論述拉回考生身上，所以考生的看法又是如何呢？在口說辯論或寫作測驗時，自己對這個議題有什麼更好的論述或看法嗎？

除了多元主題和跨領域主題的納入外，也從考古題中延伸出新穎試題。當中包含了在第 4 講堂中的企鵝構造圖和第 16 講堂中的響尾蛇構造圖，都算是在實際考試中有出現過的鯨豚類話題的延續，也更能評估出一個考生的聽力實力。此外，這次也納入了「遊戲＋歷史類」的合併主題（遊戲類話題在雅思閱讀等也會循環出現）。遊戲則採用了剛出版沒多久的 Switch 三角戰略遊戲。遊戲中包含了三個國家之間的鬥爭，玩家也必須要採取策略和取得平衡，很多決定都無關對錯，但在後續的影響卻是很顯著的。以歷史類的話題（加上一些描述手法）來納入考題確實有提升應考難度，但必然是個更靈活、新穎、貼近現齡 16-24 族群的考題。故事中三個國家「艾斯弗斯特公國」、「格林堡王國」和「聖海桑德大教國」似乎就類似三國演義中的魏、蜀和吳。當中有各個主線的故事劇情和路線，總共有五個結局。

在這些路線期間，玩家會經歷幾個場景，要求他們要評估自己和艾斯弗斯特公國與聖海桑德大教國的關係，這當中並沒有對或錯的答案，只是必須考慮當下對本國的益處。在遊戲中段時，大多數人會與聖海桑德大教國結盟以削弱艾斯弗斯特公國（類似魏國）的實力，這會包含另外的三個選擇。簡言之，在與聖海桑德大教國的其中一個合作計畫中，玩家必須要擊敗艾斯弗斯特公國的軍力，而接著使用令人畏懼的物質使艾斯弗斯特的戰船爆炸，為什麼我們會談論這個物質呢？因為這與我們和萊拉的其中一個戰役有關聯。這個可怕的物質是紫色的，而其被稱為「艾弗里克」。在那個時候，我們僅能知道其威力大到能夠毀掉艾斯弗斯特公國的戰船...。

　　但如果你選擇了芙德麗卡（主角老婆）路線，道德議題會浮現...使用「艾弗里克」會是具有道德爭議的事...尤其當瑟雷諾亞和他的團隊深入醫法院去查明真相，欲知道「艾弗里克」的組成，並且要拯救羅潔爾族時，他們最終發現了一本書《艾弗里克的運用法門》，進而得知艾弗里克是由羅潔爾族的遺體所製成。他們被萊拉逮個正著，而這就是他們開始戰鬥的時候...身為醫法院的首腦，萊拉別無選擇地要守護這個秘密...。當中搭配了更具整合性的考題，包含檢視考生歸納、配對、隱晦同義轉換能力、對應試題敘述加長的題型和檢測作者意圖的試題等等，這些都與劍橋雅思 17 調整且較難的聽力試題吻合。在其他篇中，也刪除了許多填空題，調整成延長選項敘述並包含檢測作者意圖的試題（這本書大概在 5 月份撰寫完成，劍橋雅思 17 的出版日期則在 6 月份）。劍橋雅思 17 的出題也是一個新的標誌，考生要充分掌握劍橋雅思 17 的各類題型變化，包含寫作大作文的話題和聽力考題，以充分應對這項考試。最後祝所有考生都能獲取理想成績。

韋爾 敬上

Instructions

使用說明

影子跟讀練習 MP3 002

做完題目後，除了對答案知道錯在哪外，更重要的是要修正自己聽力根本的問題，即聽力理解力和聽力專注力的修正能逐步強化本身的聽力實力，所以現在請根據聽力內容「逐個段落」、「數個段落」或「整篇」進行跟讀練習，提升在實際考場時專注聽完每個訊息、定位出關鍵考點和搭配筆記回答所有題目。Go!

Adult relationships are often very complicated, so misunderstandings generated by trivial matters can be very hard to tackle. "To see is to believe" cannot always be the solution to the disagreement because there are always different interpretations to the story. Luckily, two classics, *Middlemarch* and *Gone with the Wind* provide us with the solution that is perennially useful.

成人戀愛關係通常非常複雜，所以由瑣事引起的誤解非常難處理。「眼見為憑」不總是能成為不合的解決之道，因為每個故事總會有不一樣的詮釋。幸運的是，兩本經典鉅作《米德爾鎮的春天》和《亂世佳人》提供了我們永久有效的解決之道。

Since this topic has recently taken the spotlight in the news, we are going to probe into how two main characters in the classics solve the question by using identical methods.

既然這個主題在近期的新聞中受到了關注，我們將探討在經典著作中的兩位主角是如何使用了近似的方法解決問題。

In *Middlemarch*, when Will and Dorothea's love affair can eventually yield fruits remains unknown, and readers are able to know the answer until the very end of the book, which is quite worrisome. The anticipation can sometimes be worsened by certain events happening in the novel. The silver lining in their love affairs is aggravated by the relationship between Rosamond and Mr. Lydgate. That makes Rosamond's love slightly slanting towards Will, a guy she has been dreaming of seeing, and a guy more wonderful than her husband, Lydgate. Dorothea's visit to Rosamond's house to clear up misunderstandings between Lydgate and Rosamond and hand in an important letter of Lydgate has led to a terrible misunderstanding.

在《米德爾鎮的春天》，威爾和多蘿西亞的戀愛最終會於何時才能開花成果仍是未知數，而且讀者必須要讀到書籍非常後面才能夠得知結果，擔憂是與日俱增的。這樣的期待可能有時候受到小說中發生的特定事件而惡化。他們戀愛的一線希望更因為羅絲夢和李德蓋特之間的關係而惡化。這讓羅絲夢的愛些微向威爾偏傾倒，威爾是她一直引頸期望能見到的人，且比她丈夫更具風采。多蘿西亞前往羅絲夢家的拜訪以及澄清羅絲夢和李德蓋特之間的誤會，和一封對李德蓋特異常重要的一封信，卻導致了一個可怕的誤會。

❶ generate 產生；造成，引起
❷ disagreement 意見不合 [U]；爭吵，爭論 [C]
❸ interpretation 解釋，闡明
❹ perennially 不絕地；永駐地
❺ identical 完全相似的
❻ yield 產生（效果，收益等）
❼ anticipation 預期，期望

涵蓋多元跨領域主題，擴充知識廣度
每個主題均具深度，能反覆演練，強化思考力
「說」＋「寫」答題穩定度迅速飆升
每次應考都能獲取7.5以上的成績

· 收錄跨領域主題，例如：社會議題＋英國文學等，強化考生靈活思緒和邏輯表達，並能將高階文句流暢地運用在口說和寫作考試中。
· 此外，書籍規劃中英對照便於初中階考生自學備考。搭配影子跟讀練習法，大幅提升應考實力。

Test 1  MP3 Test 1 / MP3 004

Section 4 Questions 31-34
Complete the Notes below
Write No More Than Two Words for each answer

In *The Penguin Lessons*, numerous penguins' carcasses are discovered. To get rid of the **31.**_____ is of vital concern.

Penguins' black and white patterns are served as the function of the **32.**_____.

The thickness of penguin's **33.**_____ is 30 to 40 per square centimeter, almost triple than that of the flying birds.

Penguin's gland actually secretes the oil to make penguin's plumage **34.**_____.

Questions 35-40
Complete the diagram below
Write No More Than Two Words for each answer
Write your answers in boxes 33-40 on your answer sheet

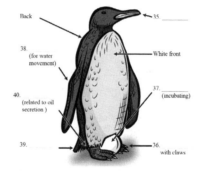

Back

38.
(for water movement)

White front

40.
(related to oil secretion)

37.
(incubating)

35.

36.
with claws

39.

鑑別度高的圖表題
加強精準定位和判斷
建構更強、更全面的「聽」＋「讀」實力
‧充分運用「聽」和「讀」之間的關聯性，收錄更多圖表題所檢視的考點，試題中包含了協助定位的關鍵字，有助於考生掌握訊息線索，面對多變的考題，在考場也能精準定位訊息考點並在腦海中分類各樣的聽力訊息，保持思緒清晰且答好每一題。（若覺得試題簡易，可遮蔽掉提示字和協助定位的語彙。）

coldness of **26.**_____ temperatures, penguin's feathers are massive that help them **27.**_____ energy and keep warm. The thickness of penguin's **28.**_____ is 30 to 40 per square centimeter, almost triple than that of the flying birds.

The size of their bill may be varied in accordance with the species. It will influence their **29.**_____ of food. Penguins which consume squid, **30.**_____ and crustaceans exhibit long and thin bills, whereas those which eat krill demonstrate the bills that are shorter and wider.

Penguins have webbed feet with visible claws, and since their feet can ensure the **31.**_____ of body temperatures, the egg of the penguin will be put between the feet for the **32.**_____ to happen, and heat loss is less likely to happen. Parents do have to keep a watchful eye for their babies.

Penguins do have flippers. The function of the flipper is similar to that of birds' wings. They assist their **33.**_____ movements. As for the tail, it has multiple functions, and its use has been downplayed by many. However, in walking, climbing, sitting, and swimming, tails play an important role.

Lastly, I want to mention about the gland that is adjacent to the tail of the penguins. The gland actually secretes the oil to make penguin's plumage **34.**_____. And in the book, the author's kindness of

washing away the body of the penguin makes it lose the ability of resistance to water. So tragically, it cannot swim back to the ocean...

| 參考答案 |

1.	pets	**2.**	adorable
3.	spotlight	**4.**	matchmaker
5.	optimistic	**6.**	emotions
7.	rare	**8.**	aquariums
9.	galvanizing	**10.**	scenery
11.	scarcity	**12.**	transpires
13.	ecological	**14.**	catastrophe
15.	suffocation	**16.**	serendipitous
17.	apartment	**18.**	vicious
19.	function	**20.**	zebras
21.	insects	**22.**	black
23.	hues	**24.**	clumsily
25.	eyesight	**26.**	ocean
27.	conserve	**28.**	plumage
29.	consumption	**30.**	fish
31.	constancy	**32.**	incubation
33.	water	**34.**	waterproof

填空測驗規劃

多一道檢視，強化拼字和聽力專注力

聽力分數迅速飆升至 9.0 佳績

‧與坊間試題和官方試題作區隔，多一道聽力填空題檢視，演練常見且必考的字彙，挖空試題更包含有與近幾年劍橋雅思官方常考的重疊語彙，有效協助考生備考，**10 倍化**聽力語感，一次就考取理想成績。

Test 3 `MP3.test 3` / `MP3 012`

Section 4
Questions 31-40

Write the correct letter, A-N, next to Questions 31-40

A Gustadolph
B Dragan
C *The Power of Salt*
D Serenoa
E Thalas
F Svarog
G Prince Roland
H Frederica
I the Grand Norzelian Mines
J Aesfrost
K Glenbrook
L the Holy State of Hyzante
M Prince Roland and Serenoa
N pink rocks

31. Important elements discovered at the cavern
32. Conduct underhanded plans to the shipment of goods
33. Has something valuable for the negotiation with two nations
34. The schemer behind the assassination
35. Return to the nation because of the imminent danger
36. Previous smart moves come back to bite him
37. One's acknowledgment that something is of vital value
38. Desire to be dominant among three nations
39. Overturn the situation during the discussion
40. Is given a mission to supervise an important site

音檔分拆，便於考生運用
可使用「完整模擬試題音檔」或「分拆音檔」
彈性搭配影子跟讀練習規劃
大幅提升實戰能力
- **Test 1**（第一回完整模擬試題音檔），亦包含MP3 001 - MP3 004。
- **Test 2**（第二回完整模擬試題音檔），亦包含MP3 005 - MP3 008。
- **Test 3**（第三回完整模擬試題音檔），亦包含MP3 009 - MP3 012。
- **Test 4**（第四回完整模擬試題音檔），亦包含MP3 013 - MP3 016。

目次CONTENTS

IELTS LISTENING Test 1

IELTS LISTENING Test 2

05 ｜Desert Heights 沙漠山莊 ❷
天氣變化和常見裝置用語

06 ｜英國文學＋社會學
《*Middlemarch*》、《*The History of Tom Jones, a Founding*》、《*Gone with the Wind*》
關於婚姻，父母該提供建議亦或是全然遵照小孩意願呢？

07 ｜英國文學＋心理學
《*1984*》、《*Middlemarch*》
誠摯單純的愛情

08 ｜英國文學＋社會學
《*Middlemarch*》、《*How Will You Measure Your Life*》、《*Where You Go Is Not Who You Will Be*》
弗烈德面臨的人生抉擇和職業的選擇

IELTS LISTENING Test 3

09 ｜Desert Heights 沙漠山莊 ❸

10 ｜英國文學＋愛情

《*Gone with the Wind*》、《*1984*》、《*Pride and Prejudice*》、
《*The History of Tom Jones, a Founding*》

11 ｜遊戲＋歷史

《*Triangle Strategy* ❶》

12 ｜遊戲＋歷史

《*Triangle Strategy* ❷》

IELTS LISTENING Test 4

13 | Desert Heights 沙漠山莊 ❹
餐具、房內裝置、病徵等用語

14 | 英國文學＋心理學
《*A Tale of Two Cities*》、
《*The History of Tom Jones, a Founding*》
德法奇夫人的毒計、貝拉斯頓夫人分別對男、女主角的陷害

15 | 英國文學＋心理學
《*Pride and Prejudice*》
伊莉莎白和達西之間的誤會

16 | 生物學
《*Walden*》、《*The Forest Unseen*》
叢林中的松鼠和其天敵

Section 1 Questions 1-10
Complete the Notes below

Write **No More Than Two Words** for each answer

Reservation for the room: contain **6 beds**

No shower room: scant **1.**_____ supply

FOOD:

- beef with **2.**_____ : 120 euro
  - nutrition value: includes plenty of potassium, which will help control **3.**_____
  - time for preparation: 20-30 minutes
- **4.**_____ eggs: two eggs 150 euros
  - nutrition value: sufficient **5.**_____
- a roasted goat: 350 euros
- must-eat: **6.**_____ ice cream
  - prevention for **7.**_____ infections

- snake meat: elevates metabolism...and increases move-ment of **8.**_____
- hot season: 30 euros for the **9.**_____ meat and 90 euros for the broth
- Fee: **10.**_____ for today and accommodation money tomorrow

試題解析

- 第 1 題，scant 1.＿＿＿＿＿＿ supply，對應到 we don't provide a shower room, since **water** is considered not plentiful, if that's ok，scant 對應到 not plentiful，故答案為 **water**。

- 第 2 題，beef with 2.＿＿＿＿＿＿，對應到 beef with **watermelon** 120 euros，聽力訊息和試題完全一致，故答案為 **watermelon**。

- 第 3 題，includes plenty of potassium, which will help control 3.＿＿＿＿＿＿，對應到 also, watermelons contain plenty of potassium, which will help regulate **muscle tissues**，contain 換成了 include，regulate 換成了 control，不過還是不會影響答案的判斷，故答案為 **muscle tissues**。

- 第 4 題，4.＿＿＿＿＿＿ eggs，對應到 **ostrich** eggs? Two eggs 150 euros，聽力訊息和試題完全一致，故答案為 **ostrich**。

- 第 5 題，sufficient 5.＿＿＿＿＿＿，對應到 that will certainly provide you with enough **protein**...，enough 換成了 sufficient，故答案為 **protein**。

● 第 6 題，**6.**＿＿＿＿＿＿＿ ice cream，對應到 **mango cactus** ice cream，聽力訊息和試題完全一致，故答案為 **mango cactus**。

● 第 7 題，prevention for **7.**＿＿＿＿＿＿＿ infections，對應到 cactuses usually act as a great way to reduce **intestine** infections...and if you order four ostrich eggs, it's on the house，reduce 換成了 prevention for 故答案為 **intestine**。

● 第 8 題，elevates metabolism...and increases movement of **8.**＿＿ ＿＿＿＿＿，對應到 snake meat elevates metabolism...and increases **blood** circulation...，前面句子並未改寫，但後面有將 circulation 換成了 movement，只是名詞片語的語序轉換，故答案為 **blood**。

● 第 9 題，30 euros for the **9.**＿＿＿＿＿＿＿ meat，對應到 what about dried **chameleon** meat and snake soup 和 we can trim the price to 30 euros for the meat，要整合這兩句的訊息才能判答，故答案為 **chameleon**。

● 第 10 題，**10.**＿＿＿＿＿＿＿ for today and accommodation money tomorrow，對應到 ❶beef with **watermelon** 120 euros，❷**ostrich** eggs? Two eggs 150 euros，❸a roasted goat for 350 euros，❹we can trim the price to 30 euros for the meat，計算後將總和相加，故答案為 **890**。

做完題目後，除了對答案知道錯的部分在哪外，更重要的是要修正自己聽力根本的問題，即聽力理解力和聽力專注力，聽力專注力的修正能逐步強化本身的聽力實力，所以現在請根據聽力內容「逐個段落」、「數個段落」或「整篇」進行跟讀練習，提升在實際考場時專注聽完每個訊息、定位出關鍵考點和搭配筆記回答完所有題目。Go!

| A |

Good afternoon, Desert Heights, How may I help you?

| A |

下午好，敝店是沙漠山莊，能幫你什麼呢？

| B |

Good afternoon, I'm with my three friends, after traversing a dry land, we need a spacious room, and money won't be a problem.

| B |

下午好，跋涉乾旱陸地後，我跟我的三位朋友需要一間寬敞的房間，錢不是問題。

| A |

Let's see...we still have a big room with six beds, but we don't provide a shower room, since **water** is considered not plentiful, if that's ok.

| A |

讓我看下...我們仍有間大房，裡頭有六張床，但是我們不提供淋浴間，因為在此水並不是那麼充沛，如果這樣可行的話。

| B |

Of course, and we are all very hungry...what do you have here?

| B |

當然，還有我們都非常餓了...你們這裡有什麼呢？

| A |

Here's the menu...please have a look.

| A |

這是菜單...請看一下。

| B |

beef with **watermelon** 120 euros?

| B |

牛肉搭西瓜要 120 歐元啊？

| A |

that's correct...and you get to sit by the fireside enjoying the dish...also, watermelons contain plenty of potassium, which will help regulate **muscle tissues**.

| A |

是啊…不過你可以坐在爐火旁享用這道菜餚…而且，西瓜含有大量的鉀，能幫助調節肌肉組織。

| B |

how long does it take to cook this meal..?

| B |

製作這道料理需要花費多少時間呢？

| A |

20-30 minutes?

| A |

20-30 分鐘。

| B |

ostrich eggs? Two eggs 150 euros?

| B |

鴕鳥蛋？兩顆要價 150 歐元啊？

| A |

that will certainly provide you with enough **protein**...

| A |

那絕對會提供你所需要的足夠蛋白質喔！...

| B |

a roasted goat for 350 euros?

| B |

烤山羊要 350 歐元啊？

| A |

that's quite a common dish visitors will order while traveling here?

| A |

來這裡旅行的旅客都會點這道相當司空見慣的菜餚。

| B |

what is the must-eat on the menu?

| B |

菜單上有什麼是必吃的料理嗎？

| A |

mango cactus ice cream...cactuses usually act as a great way to reduce **intestine** infections...and if you order four ostrich eggs, it's on the house.

| A |

芒果仙人掌冰淇淋...仙人掌通常充當為減少腸道感染的法門...而且如果你點四顆鴕鳥蛋的話，這道我們作東。

| B |

what about dried **chameleon** meat and snake soup?

| B |

那變色龍肉乾和蛇羹呢？

| A |

normally, I don't recommend people...but it wouldn't hurt to give it a try...snake meat elevates metabolism...and increases **blood** circulation...

| A |

通常我不推薦大家...但是試試看也無妨...蛇肉可以提升代謝...以及促進血液循環...

| B |

oh...it doesn't have a price...

| B |

噢！...上面沒寫價格...

| A |

normally, we go catch the alive reptiles after the customer have made the decision...

| A |

通常，我們會在客人決定好後，才進行捕捉活的爬蟲類...

| **B** |

so how much?

| **B** |

所以要多少錢呢？

| **A** |

since it's the hot season...we can trim the price to 30 euros for the meat and 90 euros for the broth...

| **A** |

既然現在是旺季...我可以將變色龍肉價格減至 30 歐元，而蛇羹則是 90 歐元...

| **B** |

what kind of snakes?

| **B** |

什麼樣的蛇類？

| **A** |

rattlesnakes...We don't use king snakes for several reasons...

| **A** |

響尾蛇...基於有些原因，所以我們不用王蛇了...

| **B** |

I'd like to order four eggs, a roasted goat, watermelon with beef, chameleon meat for four people...and a large room

| **B** |

我想要點四顆鴕鳥蛋，一頭烤山羊，牛肉搭西瓜，四人份的變色龍肉...跟一間大房間。

| **A** |

no snake?...as for the spacious room...it's 500 euros per night

| **A** |

沒有點蛇啊？...至於寬敞的房間...要每晚 500 歐元。

| **B** |

we're kind of the snake lovers...cool...

| **B** |

我們有點是蛇的愛好者...好酷

| **A** |

if you don't mind, we have to get the money for the food...first, and the room fee tomorrow...

| **A** |

如果你不介意的話，我們必須要先拿到餐點的費用，住房費的話則是明天收取...

▶▶ 填空測驗

| Instruction | MP3 001

　　現在請再聽一次音檔，並做下列的測驗，檢視自己能否完成此填空測驗和強化自己聽力能力和拼字能力，降低並修正自己漏聽到聽力訊息的機會，大幅提升應考實力。

| A |

　　Good afternoon, Desert Heights, How may I help you?

| B |

　　Good afternoon, I'm with my three friends, after **1.**＿＿＿＿＿＿ a dry land, we need a **2.**＿＿＿＿＿＿ room, and money won't be a problem.

| A |

　　Let's see...we still have a big room with six **3.**＿＿＿＿＿＿, but we don't provide a **4.**＿＿＿＿＿＿ room, since water is considered not **5.**＿＿＿＿＿＿, if that's ok.

| B |

　　Of course, and we are all very **6.**＿＿＿＿＿＿...what do you have here?

| A |

　　Here's the **7.**＿＿＿＿＿＿...please have a look.

| B |

beef with **8.**_____ 120 euros?

| A |

that's correct...and you get to sit by the **9.**_____ enjoying the dish...also, watermelons contain plenty of potassium, which will help regulate **10.**_____ tissues.

| B |

how long does it take to cook this meal..?

| A |

20-30 **11.**_____?

| B |

12._____ eggs? Two eggs 150 euros?

| A |

that will certainly provide you with enough **13.**_____...

| B |

a roasted **14.**_____ for 350 euros?

| A |

that's quite a common dish **15.**_____ will order while traveling here?

| B |

what is the must-eat on the menu?

| A |

16._____ cactus ice cream...cactuses usually act as a great way to reduce 17._____ infections...and if you order four ostrich eggs, it's on the house.

| B |

what about dried 18._____ meat and snake soup?

| A |

normally, I don't recommend people...but it wouldn't hurt to give it a try...snake meat elevates 19._____...and increases blood 20._____...

| B |

oh...it doesn't have a price...

| A |

normally, we go catch the alive 21._____ after the customer have made the 22._____...

| B |

so how much?

Test 1
Test 2
Test 3
Test 4

| A |

since it's the hot **23.**_____...we can trim the price to 30 euros for the meat and 90 euros for the **24.**_____...

| B |

what kind of snakes?

| A |

25._____...We don't use **26.**_____ snakes for several reasons...

| B |

I'd like to order four eggs, a roasted goat, watermelon with beef, chameleon meat for four people...and a large room

| A |

no snake?...as for the spacious room...it's 500 euros per night

| B |

we're kind of the snake **27.**_____...cool...

| A |

if you don't mind, we have to get the **28.**_____ for the food...first, and the room **29.**_____ **30.**_____ ...

| 參考答案 |

1. traversing
2. spacious
3. beds
4. shower
5. plentiful
6. hungry
7. menu
8. watermelon
9. fireside
10. muscle
11. minutes
12. ostrich
13. protein
14. goat
15. visitors
16. mango
17. intestine
18. chameleon
19. metabolism
20. circulation
21. reptiles
22. decision
23. season
24. broth
25. rattlesnakes
26. king
27. lovers
28. money
29. fee
30. tomorrow

Section 2
Questions 11-20

Write the correct letter, A-J, next to Questions 11-20

A possess power and money that can easily take down someone

B cannot stomach the behavior of timidity

C placate the embarrassment during one's visit

D give someone a sense of security

E witness a behavior that cannot be tolerated in the society

F a vital document related to someone

G dissemination of rumor details

H arm with indifference when facing someone

I reluctance to go to the birthday party

J breed resentment against someone

---

11. Scarlett
12. Rhett
13. Melanie
14. India and Mrs. Elsing
15. Will
16. Dorothea
17. Rosamond
18. Lydgate
19. Ashley
20. India, Archie, and Mrs. Elsing

Test 2

Test 3

Test 4

影子跟讀練習 MP3 002

做完題目後，除了對答案知道錯的部分在哪外，更重要的是要修正自己聽力根本的問題，即聽力理解力和聽力專注力，聽力專注力的修正能逐步強化本身的聽力實力，所以現在請根據聽力內容「逐個段落」、「數個段落」或「整篇」進行跟讀練習，提升在實際考場時專注聽完每個訊息、定位出關鍵考點和搭配筆記回答完所有題目。Go!

Adult relationships are often very complicated, so misunderstandings generated by trivial matters can be very hard to tackle. "To see is to believe" cannot always be the solution to the disagreement because there are always different interpretations to the story. Luckily, two classics, *Middlemarch* and *Gone with the Wind* provide us with the solution that is perennially useful.

成人戀愛關係通常非常複雜，所以由瑣事引起的誤解非常難處理。「眼見為憑」不總是能成為不合的解決之道，因為每個故事總會有不一樣的詮釋。幸運的是，兩本經典鉅作《米德爾鎮的春天》和《亂世佳人》提供了我們永久有效的解決之道。

Since this topic has recently taken the spotlight in the news, we are going to probe into how two main characters in the classics solve the question by using identical methods.

既然這個主題在近期的新聞中受到了關注，我們將探討在經典著作中的兩位主角是如何使用了近似的方法解決問題。

In *Middlemarch*, when Will and Dorothea's love affair can eventually yield fruits remains unknown, and readers are able to know the answer until the very end of the book, which is quite worrisome. The anticipation can sometimes be worsened by certain events happening in the novel. The silver lining in their love affairs is aggravated by the relationship between Rosamond and Mr. Lydgate. That makes Rosamond's love slightly slanting towards Will, a guy she has been dreaming of seeing, and a guy more wonderful than her husband, Lydgate. Dorothea's visit to Rosamond's house to clear up misunderstandings between Lydgate and Rosamond and hand in an important letter of Lydgate has led to a terrible misunderstanding.

在《米德爾鎮的春天》，威爾和多羅西亞的戀愛最終會於何時才能開花成果仍是未知數，而且讀者必須要讀到書籍非常後面才能夠得知結果，擔憂是與日俱增的。這樣的期待可能有時候受到小說中發生的特定事件而惡化。他們戀愛的一線希望更因為羅絲夢和李德蓋特之間的關係而惡化。這讓羅絲夢的愛些微向威爾這頭傾倒，威爾是她一直引頸期望能見到的人，且比她丈夫更具風采。多羅西亞前往羅絲夢家的拜訪以及澄清羅絲夢和李德蓋特之間的誤會，和一封對李德蓋特異常重要的一封信，卻導致了一個可怕的誤會。

❶ generate 產生；造成，引起
❷ disagreement 意見不合 [U]；爭吵，爭論 [C]
❸ interpretation 解釋；闡明
❹ perennially 不絕地；永駐地
❺ identical 完全相似的
❻ yield 產生（效果，收益等）
❼ anticipation 預期，期望

❽ aggravate 加重；增劇

❾ slightly 輕微地；稍微地

❿ slant 使傾斜，使傾向

Upon entering the house, Dorothea unexpectedly finds Rosamond sitting next to Will, with tears in her eyes and with Will's body leaning towards Rosamond...is that what Dorothea sees...? To see is to believe...? Rosamond is desperately in need of a shoulder to cry on because of her marital problems with her husband...and as to Will, till chapter 77, he cannot be..., he only loves Dorothea...so how can Dorothea properly respond the situation when she meets Rosamond...by resenting Rosamond for stealing Will from her? Dorothea can easily do so by taking the revenge upon Rosamond given her status and wealth in the novel. As for Will, he now holds a grudge against Rosamond, and that he will never have a chance with Dorothea...

在進房後，多蘿西亞出乎意料之外地發現羅絲夢坐在威爾身旁，眼中泛著淚，還有威爾的身體向羅絲夢傾倒...這真是多蘿西亞所見到的嗎...？眼見為憑...？羅絲夢迫切地需要一個肩膀以宣洩情緒，因為她自己本身與丈夫之間的婚姻問題...而關於威爾，直到第 77 章，他不可能會如此，他只愛著多蘿西亞...所以當多蘿西亞再遇見羅絲夢時，又該如何以最合適的方式去應對這個情況呢？...去憎恨羅絲夢從她手中奪走威爾嗎？有鑑於她在小說中的地位和財富，多蘿西亞要進行報復的話可以說是輕而易舉。而關於威爾，他現在對羅絲夢懷恨在心，這意謂著他跟多蘿西亞能在一起的希望將化為泡影。

During the second visit to the house, Rosamond is covered with a towel and uses her aloofness to arm herself...she is totally not ready for Dorothea's visit...as for Dorothea, she finds the talk with Rosamond surprisingly difficult, and she wills herself not to generate any tears in the eyes...then she speaks...Dorothea's sincerity and her generosity to help Lydgate have weakened Rosamond's fear and timidness in confronting with what actually happened that day...Dorothea's spontaneity and empathy are also the drive to Rosamond's full closure...it's not what you saw that day...Will wanted to tell me that how he loves another woman, that he will never love me, and now Will is resenting me that you misunderstand him...were it not for Dorothea's personality, she would not have the relationship with Will and would continue mistakenly thinking he loves Rosamond...there won't be a happy denouement...

在第二次拜訪時，羅絲夢以一條毛巾包裹著，並且用她自我的冷漠武裝起自己...，對於多羅西亞的拜訪，她顯然完全沒準備好...至於多羅西亞，她察覺到要開口跟羅絲夢說話是多麼困難，她以自我意志控制自己眼睛不要湧現眼淚...接著，她開口說話...多羅西亞的誠摯和慷慨大方地幫助李德蓋特已經弱化了羅絲夢的恐懼和膽怯，以至於她能面對那天實際發生的情況了...多羅西亞的自然流露和同理心也是驅使羅絲夢能夠全然招供的原因...一切都不是妳所看到的那樣...威爾想要告訴我他愛著另一個女人，而他從未喜愛過我，然後現在威爾因為妳誤會他而對我懷恨在心...若不是多羅西亞的個性，她沒辦法與威爾在一起，而是持續地誤解威爾愛著羅絲夢...那樣的話，完美的結局就不會發生了。

❶ unexpectedly 未料到地，意外地

❷ desperately 絕望地；不顧一切地

❸ marital 婚姻的；夫妻的

❹ grudge 怨恨；妒忌

❺ aloofness 冷漠，高傲

❻ generosity 寬宏大量；慷慨

❼ weaken 削弱，減弱

❽ spontaneity 自發性；自然發生

❾ empathy 同理心

❿ denouement（小說、戲劇等的）結局

In *Gone with the Wind*, the development of the story shares an identical vein. When Scarlett is in the arms of Ashley, feeling safe, they accidentally get caught by India, Archie, and Mrs. Elsing. Scarlett even has a whimsical notion that a friendly gesture between them to be mistakenly thought of as "an adultery". This obviously cannot be good because India and Mrs. Elsing will make a parade of what they descried a few minutes ago, and wouldn't mind trumpeting the juicy story to all the neighborhood.

在《亂世佳人》中，故事的發展有著異曲同工之處。當思嘉莉倚在艾希禮的臂膀間，感到安穩時，他們卻意外地被英迪亞、安爾琴和埃爾辛太太撞見。思嘉莉甚至突發奇想，這僅是他們之間的友誼舉動，卻要被誤解成是「通姦」。這顯然不妙，因為英迪亞和埃爾辛太太會誇耀地描述幾分鐘前所見之事，且不介意大肆渲染這個富刺激性的故事到所有街坊中。

How does Scarlett's husband, Rhett respond to the adultery...he can endure the extramarital affair, but he cannot seem to tolerate cowardice...no matter how awkward it sounds, Scarlett has to go to Ashley's birthday party...what's Melanie's viewpoints about the rumor between her husband and Scarlett...

思嘉莉的丈夫瑞德又是如何回應這個通姦呢？...他可以忍受外遇這件事，但他似乎無法忍受膽小如鼠的行為...不論聽起來是多麼蠢，思嘉莉必須要去參加艾希禮的生日派對...媚蘭對於她老公和思嘉莉之前的八卦的觀點又是如何呢...？

Fortunately, the birthday party begins with the good news...Melanie cordially welcomes Scarlett's visit thus, softening the embarrassment...plus, she won't believe such a thing. After all, it's a rumor. Throughout the novel, Melanie is the person who knows Scarlett too well, so she won't believe such a thing...at the very end of the novel, even Scarlett admits why it takes her so long to realize that she doesn't love Ashley...it is Melanie's kindness, candidness, and courage that prevents the rumor or the scandal from getting worsened or widespread...only with these noble traits, can Melanie and Dorothea get the desired result...revenge and other negative characteristics won't be the cure to all situations...

幸運的是，生日派對是以好消息的方式為開端...媚蘭熱情地歡迎思嘉莉的拜訪，因而軟化了尷尬的局面...再說，她不會相信那樣的事情。畢竟，那只是八卦。小說通篇，媚蘭對思嘉莉太了解了，所以她不可能相信那樣的事情...在小說的最尾端，甚至思嘉莉坦承為什麼花費她這麼久才意識到她自己不愛艾希禮...是媚蘭的善良、坦率和勇氣，讓八卦或醜聞不會更為惡化或廣為流傳...也只有有著這些高貴的特質，媚蘭和多羅西亞才能得到稱心如意的結果...復仇和其他負面特質對所有情況來說不會是解方。

❶ adultery 通姦；通姦行為

❷ parade 炫示，誇耀

❸ descry 看見，辨認出

❹ trumpet 大力宣傳

❺ awkward 笨拙的；不熟練的

❻ cordially 熱誠地，誠摯地

❼ soften 使變柔軟

❽ worsen（使）惡化

❾ widespread 普遍的；廣泛的

❿ negative 否認的；反面的

試題解析

- 第 **11** 題，Scarlett 符合選項 reluctance to go to the birthday party，對應到 no matter how awkward it sounds, Scarlett has to go to Ashley's birthday party...，Scarlett 因為醜聞事件而覺得參加生日派對是件很尷尬的事情，所以不願意前往，但是瑞德覺得不去的話更奇怪，故答案要選 **I**。

- 第 **12** 題，Rhett 符合選項 cannot stomach the behavior of timidity，對應到 he can endure the extramarital affair, but he cannot seem to tolerate cowardice...，當中 stomach = tolerate，cowardice = timidity，指瑞德無法忍受行為膽怯，故答案要選 **B**。

- 第 **13** 題，Melanie 符合選項 placate the embarrassment during one's visit，對應到 Melanie cordially welcomes Scarlett's visit thus, softening the embarrassment...，當中 placate = soften，表示化解了尷尬情況，故答案要選 **C**。

- 第 **14** 題，India and Mrs. Elsing 符合選項 dissemination of rumor details，對應到 This obviously cannot be good because India and Mrs. Elsing will make a parade of what they descried a few minutes ago, and wouldn't mind trumpeting the juicy story to all the neighborhood，當中 dissemination of rumor details = trumpeting the juicy，指不介意「大肆渲染/散佈」這個富刺激性的故事到所有街坊中，故答案要選 **G**。

- **第 15 題**，Will 符合選項 breed resentment against someone，對應到 As for Will, he now holds a grudge against Rosamond, and that he will never have a chance with Dorothea...，當中 breed resentment against someone = holds a grudge against，威爾現在對羅絲夢懷恨在心，這意謂著他跟多羅西亞能在一起的希望將化為泡影，故答案要選 **J**。

- **第 16 題**，Dorothea 符合選項 possess power and money that can easily take down someone，對應到 Dorothea can easily do so by taking the revenge upon Rosamond given her status and wealth in the novel，當中 status and wealth = power and money，在小說中，多羅西亞的地位和財富，讓其可以輕而易舉的這麼做以進行報復，而當時羅絲夢的丈夫甚至還欠下一大筆債，故答案要選 **A**。

- **第 17 題**，Rosamond 符合選項 arm with indifference when facing someone，對應到 Rosamond is covered with a towel and uses her aloofness to arm herself...she is totally not ready for Dorothea's visit，當中 indifference = aloofness，指在第二次拜訪時，羅絲夢以一條毛巾包裹著，並且用她自我的冷漠武裝起自己...故答案要選 **H**。

- **第 18 題**，Lydgate 符合選項 a vital document related to someone，對應到 hand in an important letter of Lydgate has led to a terrible misunderstanding，當中 important letter = vital document，指的是重要信件，故答案要選 **F**。

- **第 19 題**，Ashley 符合選項 give someone a sense of security，對應到 When Scarlett is in the arms of Ashley, feeling safe, they accidentally get caught by India, Archie, and Mrs. Elsing，當中 feeling safe = a sense of security，在艾希禮懷抱中，感到安全，指的就是讓其有安全感，故答案要選 **D**。

- **第 20 題**，India, Archie, and Mrs. Elsing 符合選項 witness a behavior that cannot be tolerated in the society，對應到 They accidentally get caught by India, Archie, and Mrs. Elsing. Scarlett even has a whimsical notion that a friendly gesture between them to be mistakenly thought of as "an adultery"，adultery = a behavior that cannot be tolerated，這是較隱晦的改寫，但 adultery 就是社會所無法容忍的事，故答案要選 **E**。

Instruction | MP3 002

現在請再聽一次音檔，並做下列的測驗，檢視自己能否完成此填空測驗和強化自己聽力能力和拼字能力，降低並修正自己漏聽到聽力訊息的機會，大幅提升應考實力。

Adult relationships are often very **1.**_____ , so misunderstandings generated by **2.**_____ matters can be very hard to tackle. "To see is to believe" cannot always be the solution to the **3.**_____ because there are always different **4.**_____ to the story. Luckily, two classics, *Middlemarch* and *Gone with the Wind* provide us with the **5.**_____ that is perennially useful.

Since this topic has recently taken the **6.**_____ in the news, we are going to probe into how two main **7.**_____ in the classics solve the question by using **8.**_____ methods.

In *Middlemarch*, when Will and Dorothea's love affair can eventually yield **9.**_____ remains unknown, and readers are able to know the answer until the very end of the book, which is quite **10.**_____. The anticipation can sometimes be **11.**_____ by certain events happening in the novel. The silver lining in their love affairs is aggravated by the relationship between Rosamond and Mr. Lydgate. That makes Rosamond's love **12.**_____ slanting towards Will, a guy she has been dreaming of seeing, and a guy more wonderful than her husband, Lydgate.

Dorothea's visit to Rosamond's house to clear up misunderstandings between Lydgate and Rosamond and hand in an important letter of Lydgate has led to a **13.**_____ misunderstanding.

Upon entering the house, Dorothea **14.**_____ finds Rosamond sitting next to Will, with tears in her eyes and with Will's body leaning towards Rosamond...is that what Dorothea sees...? To see is to believe...? Rosamond is **15.**_____ in need of a shoulder to cry on because of her marital problems with her husband...and as to Will, till chapter 77, he cannot be..., he only loves Dorothea...so how can Dorothea properly respond the situation when she meets Rosamond...by resenting Rosamond for stealing Will from her? Dorothea can easily do so by taking the **16.**_____ upon Rosamond given her status and **17.**_____ in the novel. As for Will, he now holds a **18.**_____ against Rosamond, and that he will never have a chance with Dorothea...

During the second visit to the house, Rosamond is covered with a **19.**_____ and uses her **20.**_____ to arm herself...she is totally not ready for Dorothea's visit...as for Dorothea, she finds the talk with Rosamond surprisingly difficult, and she wills herself not to generate any **21.**_____ in the eyes...then she speaks...Dorothea's sincerity and her **22.**_____ to help Lydgate have weakened Rosamond's fear and **23.**_____ in confronting with what actually happened that day...Dorothea's **24.**_____ and empathy are also the drive to Rosamond's full closure...it's not what you saw that day...Will wanted to tell me that how he loves another woman,

Test 1

Test 2

Test 3

Test 4

that he will never love me, and now Will is resenting me that you misunderstand him...were it not for Dorothea's **25._____**, she would not have the relationship with Will and would continue mistakenly thinking he loves Rosamond...there won't be a happy **26._____**...

In *Gone with the Wind*, the development of the story shares an identical vein. When Scarlett is in the arms of Ashley, feeling safe, they accidentally get caught by India, Archie, and Mrs. Elsing. Scarlett even has a **27._____** notion that a friendly gesture between them to be mistakenly thought of as "an **28._____**". This obviously cannot be good because India and Mrs. Elsing will make a parade of what they **29._____** a few minutes ago, and wouldn't mind **30._____** the juicy story to all the neighborhood.

How does Scarlett's husband, Rhett respond to the adultery...he can endure the **31._____** affair, but he cannot seem to tolerate **32._____**...no matter how awkward it sounds, Scarlett has to go to Ashley's birthday party...what's Melanie's viewpoints about the rumor between her husband and Scarlett...Fortunately, the birthday party begins with the good news...Melanie cordially welcomes Scarlett's visit thus, softening the **33._____**...plus, she won't believe such a thing. After all, it's a rumor. Throughout the novel, Melanie is the person who knows Scarlett too well, so she won't believe such a thing...at the very end of the novel, even Scarlett admits why it takes for so long to realize that she doesn't love Ashley...it is Melanie's kindness, candidness, and **34._____** that prevents the rumor or the **35.**_____ from getting worsened or widespread...only with these **36.**_____ traits, can Melanie and Dorothea get the desired result...revenge and other negative characteristics won't be the cure to all situations...

| 參考答案 |

1. complicated	**2.** trivial
3. disagreement	**4.** interpretations
5. solution	**6.** spotlight
7. characters	**8.** identical
9. fruits	**10.** worrisome
11. worsened	**12.** slightly
13. terrible	**14.** unexpectedly
15. desperately	**16.** revenge
17. wealth	**18.** grudge
19. towel	**20.** aloofness
21. tears	**22.** generosity
23. timidness	**24.** spontaneity
25. personality	**26.** denouement
27. whimsical	**28.** adultery
29. descried	**30.** trumpeting
31. extramarital	**32.** cowardice
33. embarrassment	**34.** courage
35. scandal	**36.** noble

Section 3
Questions 21-30

Write the correct letter, A-J, next to Questions 21-30
(You may use the letter, more than once)

A Black George
B Tom Jones
C Allworthy
D Thwackum
E Square
F wench
G Blifil
H Sophia
I Blifil and Thwackum
J the little horse

21. make a request that includes handing in a document
22. has a conspicuous injury on the chest
23. make a decision that can make a whole family suffer
24. descry something occurring in the bush
25. camouflage an event for a later use
26. has sex with someone in the shrub
27. has the right that can waive someone's benefits
28. eventually get no less than 500 pounds
29. whose feelings towards someone are swayed
30. toss all the things in the wallet

做完題目後，除了對答案知道錯的部分在哪外，更重要的是要修正自己聽力根本的問題，即聽力理解力和聽力專注力，聽力專注力的修正能逐步強化本身的聽力實力，所以現在請根據聽力內容「逐個段落」、「數個段落」或「整篇」進行跟讀練習，提升在實際考場時專注聽完每個訊息、定位出關鍵考點和搭配筆記回答完所有題目。Go!

We have been taught that one has to be grateful, and there is even a perennial saying that life is all about give and take, or give and you shall receive. Possessing a kind heart and being willing to give are good for human welfare, and sometimes you can benefit from things you had done. However, this is not usually the case, as can be seen in *The History of Tom Jones, a Founding*. So let's take a quick look at book three, chapter 8...a childish incident...

我們受到的教育教導我們人必須要感恩，甚至有種不朽的說法是，生命全是施與受，或是給予你才能有所獲得。擁有一顆善良的心以及願意給予對於人類福祉來說是有益的，而有時候你能從你先前的所做所為當中獲益。然而，事情的發展卻通常不是如此，如同你在《湯姆・瓊斯》當中所目睹的事件演變。所以讓我們很快地看一下第三卷第八章...一個孩童時期的事件。

It is about a gift, the horse that Mr. Allworthy gave to Tom as a compensation. Tom later sells it in the neighboring fair. Thwackum, Tom's master, immediately asks him about the money, but Tom refuses to answer. Tom is then taken to another room, getting the same question from his father, Mr. Allworthy.

事件是關於一個由歐渥希所贈與湯姆的禮物，以作為補償。湯姆卻於稍後將其於鄰里的市集中兜售掉了。史瓦坎，也就是湯姆的老師，立即詢問他關於錢的去處，但是湯姆卻拒絕回應。湯姆接著被帶到另一間房，被歐渥希，也就是其父親，詢問了同樣的問題。

Legitimate criticisms from Mr. Allworthy, Thwackum, some readers, might include not showing enough appreciation of the gift from father to son, or using the sold money for other purposes, making Tom carry an unfair stigma.

歐渥希、史瓦坎以及有些讀者對於這事件的正當批評，可能包含了其並未顯示出父親贈送禮物給兒子的充分感激之情，或是將賣馬的錢用到其他用途上頭，讓湯姆背負著不公平的罪名。

However, the money actually goes to the gamekeeper whom Mr. Allworthy discharges. Tom helps the poor, those in need, and with the money, the gamekeeper and his family can endure coldness and hunger for a while...how can little Tom possess such a good temperament? How does he get in return? Will good deeds generate bad consequences?

然而，販售小馬所獲得的錢實際上卻到了被歐渥希所辭退的看守人的手中。湯姆幫助了貧窮、需要幫助的人，而有了那筆錢，看守人和他的家人可以在飢寒受凍中撐過一段時日...小湯姆怎麼能夠有這個善良的本質呢？他又會從看守人那裡得到什麼樣的回報呢？善行是否會招致惡果呢？

❶ grateful 感謝的，感激的

❷ possess 擁有，持有

❸ childish 幼稚的；傻氣的

❹ compensation 補償；賠償

❺ legitimate 正當的，合理的

❻ criticism 批評；評論

❼ appreciation 欣賞，鑑賞

❽ purpose 目的，意圖

❾ stigma 恥辱，汙名

❿ discharge 釋放；解僱 [U]

We have to jump to book 6, chapter 10...The development of the story is actually bad for Tom...Blifil is accusing Tom of his ingratitude to Mr. Allworthy, Blifil's uncle. Blifil's narration comes across as an attempt to knock down Tom, but Tom does do several things that are morally questionable...

對此我們要跳至第六卷，第十章...故事的發展實際上對於湯姆是不利的...布里菲正向歐渥希，也就是他的舅舅，控訴湯姆的忘恩負義。布里菲的敘述體現了他試圖將湯姆擊垮之舉，但是湯姆確實犯了幾件道德上備受爭議之事。

Tom engages in a sexual discourse in the bush, which accidentally gets witnessed by Blifil and Thwackum...Blifil actually saw the girl, but he didn't know who in a far distance. Thwackum didn't witness the wench, but he knew there was something going on in the bush. He desperately wanted to know who that was, forgetting the fact that Blifil was getting hit by Tom.

湯姆在灌木叢中與人發生性行為，卻意外地被布里菲和史瓦坎撞見…布里菲確實看到了那個女子，但是他距離太遠了，所以無法得知女子真實身分。史瓦坎並未看到那個蕩婦，但是他知道在灌木叢中一定有甚麼事情發生。他迫切地想要知道到底是誰在那裡，以至於全然忘記了布里菲正受到湯姆的攻擊。

Blifil tells the whole juicy details to Allworthy, making Allworthy wonder is he raising a monster…Thwackum is soon called by Allworthy, not for the confirmation of the story, but for examination of all the facts. Thwackum shows the proof on his breast, the visible wound resulting from Tom's hitting. Concealment of things like this makes Blifil, the person of noble character, aggravating Allworthy's impressions of Tom.

布里菲將這整個富刺激性的細節告知歐渥希，歐渥希思考著，自己是否養了一個兇惡之徒…史瓦坎立即受到歐渥希的傳喚，並不是要確認事情的真實性，而是要檢視所有事證。史瓦坎秀出胸口上的證據，導因於湯姆毆打的傷口仍清晰可見。隱藏像這樣的事不說讓布里菲成了高貴品格的人，惡化了歐渥希對湯姆的印象。

❶ ingratitude 忘恩負義
❷ narration 敘述，講述 [U]
❸ questionable 可疑的；成問題的
❹ sexual 性慾的
❺ accidentally 偶然地；意外地
❻ witness 目擊
❼ wench 蕩婦；妓女

❽ juicy 富刺激性的

❾ confirmation 確定；確證

❿ concealment 隱藏；隱瞞

Tom's unaware of slander from Blifil, and if he cannot come up with sufficient reasons for all those indictments, he will be banished from Allworthy's sight. Given all unfavorable conditions, Tom can say nothing. He is given with a paper that includes enough money for him to live a decent living. As for the paper, it's no less than 500 pounds.

湯姆仍未察覺出布里菲對自己的誹謗，而如果他不能構想所有這些控訴的正當原因，他會被歐渥希逐出家門。考量到所有不利的情況，湯姆無話可說。他拿到一張紙上頭包含了足夠的錢讓他往後能有像樣的生活。而這張紙的價值則不少於 500 磅。

"Misfortunes seldom come single." He is drowning in sorrow, and in that violent agony, he tosses all the things in the pocket. Now he cannot find anything else in the pocket, including the money. While searching for the money, he encounters Black George, the gamekeeper, the one who owes Tom a great favor, since Tom once sells the little horse to keep Black George and his family members from starvation. Black George acts like a good friend, who examines every place with scrutiny, telling Tom that lost items are about to be found. However, they cannot find anything because it's in Black George's pocket.

「福無雙至，禍不單行。」他沉浸於悲傷中，在極度苦痛之中，他將口袋中的所有東西都丟棄了。現在，他無法找到口袋裡的任何東西了，包含那筆錢。在找尋那筆錢的時候，他碰見黑喬治，也就是看守人，欠湯姆一個大人情的人，因為湯姆曾販售小馬讓黑喬治和家人免受飢餓。黑喬治表現的像是湯姆的好友，陪同他仔細地檢視每個地方，告訴湯姆遺失的東西都將會找到。然後，他們卻搜尋未果，因為東西在黑喬治的口袋裡。

Black George even hesitates over...when Tom is asking him for a big favor after the search. He fears that it might be something too difficult or it involves lending him the money, feeling relived to know that Tom only wants him to deliver a letter to Sophia. Black George then walks away with the money, leaving Tom there not knowing his future.

在搜尋結束後，當湯姆請他幫一個大忙時...黑喬治甚至猶豫著...。黑喬治害怕可能會是很困難的請求或者事牽涉到要向他借錢，在得知湯姆只是要他將一封信遞交給蘇菲亞後就感到如釋重負。黑喬治接著帶著錢離開了，留下湯姆在原地，不知道自己未來在哪。

How come? Tom is getting the "ingratitude" instead of the "gratitude"...like what's stated in other classics, how can one ever believe in human goodness?

為什麼結果會是如此呢？湯姆得到的「忘恩負義」而不是「感激」...就像是在其他經典中所述，一個人要如何再去相信人的良善美好呢？

❶ unaware 未察覺到的
❷ slander 誹謗，詆毀
❸ sufficient 足夠的，充分的

❹ indictment 控告，告發

❺ decent 體面的；像樣的

❻ misfortune 不幸；惡運

❼ starvation 飢餓；挨餓

❽ scrutiny 詳細的檢查

❾ hesitate 躊躇；猶豫

❿ goodness 善良；仁慈

試題解析

- 第 **21** 題，make a request that includes handing in a document，對應到 He fears that it might be something too difficult or it involves lending him the money, feeling relived to know that Tom only wants him to deliver a letter to Sophia，指湯姆所提出的要求，即遞交一封信給蘇菲亞（在聽力訊息末才出現這訊息），故答案要選 **B** Tom Jones。

- 第 **22** 題，has a conspicuous injury on the chest，對應到 Thwackum shows the proof on his breast, the visible wound resulting from Tom's hitting，當中 a conspicuous injury = the visible wound，顯著的傷口就等同於傷口明顯可見，故答案要選 **D** Thwackum。

- 第 **23** 題，make a decision that can make a whole family suffer，對應到 However, the money actually goes to the gamekeeper whom Mr. Allworthy discharges，當中 discharges = make a whole family suffer 為較隱晦的同義表達，歐渥希裁掉 gamekeeper，就讓他和他們全家飢寒受凍，故答案要選 **C** Allworthy。

- 第 **24** 題，descry something occurring in the bush，對應到 Tom engages in a sexual discourse in the bush, which accidentally gets witnessed by Blifil and Thwackum，當中 descry something occurring = gets witnessed，descry 為高階字彙表示「看見，辨認出」，故答案要選 **I** Blifil and Thwackum。

- 第 25 題，camouflage an event for a later use，對應到 Concealment of things like this makes Blifil, the person of noble character, aggravating Allworthy's impressions of Tom，當中 camouflage an event for a later use = Concealment of things like this，在事發當下，Blifil 隱瞞不說，而是到了更有利的時候，一舉讓湯姆垮掉，故答案要選 **G** Blifil。

- 第 26 題，has sex with someone in the shrub，對應到 Tom engages in a sexual discourse in the bush，當中 has sex with someone = engages in a sexual discourse，指的就是發生性行為，故答案要選 **B** Tom Jones。

- 第 27 題，has the right that can waive someone's benefits，對應到 if he cannot come up with sufficient reasons for all those indictments, he will be banished from Allworthy's sight，當中 waive someone's benefits = banished，為較隱晦的同義表達，將湯姆驅逐趕出家門，就表示湯姆日後要自食其力，也不再具有任何富家公子所能享有的權利了，故答案要選 **C** Allworthy。

- 第 28 題，eventually get no less than 500 pounds，對應到 However, they cannot find anything because it's in Black George's pocket，湯姆是得到這筆錢，但題目是說最終拿到這筆錢的人，所以要選黑喬治，黑喬治將這張 paper 放進自己口袋裡，故答案要選 **A** Black George。

● **第 29 題**，whose feelings towards someone are swayed，對應到 Blifil tells the whole juicy details to Allworthy, making Allworthy wonder is he raising a monster... ，當中 feelings towards someone are swayed = wonder，wonder 指的就是對某人的感受動搖了，所以才會有後來將湯姆逐出家門一事，故答案要選 **C** Allworthy。

● **第 30 題**，toss all the things in the wallet，對應到 He is drowning in sorrow, and in that violent agony, he tosses all the things in the pocket，pocket 換成了 wallet，故答案要選 **B** Tom Jones。

▶▶ 填空測驗

現在請再聽一次音檔，並做下列的測驗，檢視自己能否完成此填空測驗和強化自己聽力能力和拼字能力，降低並修正自己漏聽到聽力訊息的機會，大幅提升應考實力。現在請再聽一次音檔，並做下列的測驗，檢視自己能否完成此填空測驗和強化自己聽力能力和拼字能力，降低並修正自己漏聽到聽力訊息的機會，大幅提升應考實力。

We have been taught that one has to be **1.**_____, and there is even a perennial saying that life is all about give and take, or give and you shall receive. Possessing a kind heart and being willing to give are good for the human welfare, and sometimes you can benefit from things you had done. However, this is not usually the case, as can be seen in *The History of Tom Jones, a Founding*. So let's take a quick look at book three, chapter 8...a **2.**_____ incident...

It is about a gift, the **3.**_____ that Mr. Allworthy gave to Tom as a **4.**_____. Tom later sells it in the neighboring fair. Thwackum, Tom's **5.**_____, immediately asks him about the **6.**_____, but Tom refuses to answer. Tom is then taken to another room, getting the same question from his father, Mr. Allworthy.

7._____ criticisms from Mr. Allworthy, Thwackum, some readers, might include not showing enough **8.**_____ of the gift from father to son, or using the sold money for other purposes, making

Tom carry an unfair **9.**_____.

However, the money actually goes to the **10.**_____ whom Mr. Allworthy discharges. Tom helps the poor, those in need, and with the money, the gamekeeper and his family can endure coldness and **11.**_____ for a while...how can little Tom possess such a good **12.**_____? How does he get in return? Will good **13.**_____ generate bad consequences?

We have to jump to book 6, chapter 10...The development of the story is actually bad for Tom...Blifil is accusing Tom of his **14.**_____ to Mr. Allworthy, Blifil's uncle. Blifil's **15.**_____ comes across as an attempt to knock down Tom, but Tom does do several things that are morally questionable...

Tom engages in a sexual **16.**_____ in the bush, which accidentally gets witnessed by Blifil and Thwackum...Blifil actually saw the girl, but he didn't know who in a far **17.**_____. Thwackum didn't witness the **18.**_____, but he knew there was something going on in the bush. He desperately wanted to know who that was, forgetting the fact that Blifil was getting hit by Tom.

Blifil tells the whole **19.**_____ details to Allworthy, making Allworthy wonder is he raising a **20.**_____...Thwackum is soon called by Allworthy, not for the **21.**_____ of the story, but for **22.**_____ of all the facts. Thwackum shows the proof on his breast, the **23.**_____ wound resulting from Tom's hitting. **24.**__

_____ of things like this makes Blifil, the person of noble character, aggravating Allworthy's **25.**_____ of Tom.

Tom's unaware of **26.**_____ from Blifil, and if he cannot come up with sufficient reasons for all those **27.**_____, he will be banished from Allworthy's sight. Given all **28.**_____ conditions, Tom can say nothing. He is given with a paper that includes enough money for him to live a decent living. As for the paper, it's no less than 500 pounds.

"**29.**_____ seldom come single." He is drowning in sorrow, and in that violent agony, he tosses all the things in the pocket. Now he cannot find anything else in the pocket, including the money. While searching for the money, he encounters Black George, the gamekeeper, the one who owes Tom a great favor, since Tom once sells the little horse to keep Black George and his family members from **30.**_____. Black George acts like a good friend, who examines every place with scrutiny, telling Tom that lost items are about to be found. However, they cannot find anything because it's in Black George's pocket.

Black George even **31.**_____ over...when Tom is asking him for a big favor after the search. He fears that it might be something too difficult or it involves lending him the money, feeling **32.**_____ to know that Tom only wants him to deliver a letter to Sophia. Black George then walks away with the money, leaving Tom there not knowing his future......

參考答案

1. grateful	**2.** childish
3. horse	**4.** compensation
5. master	**6.** money
7. Legitimate	**8.** appreciation
9. stigma	**10.** gamekeeper
11. hunger	**12.** temperament
13. deeds	**14.** ingratitude
15. narration	**16.** discourse
17. distance	**18.** wench
19. juicy	**20.** monster
21. confirmation	**22.** examination
23. visible	**24.** Concealment
25. impressions	**26.** slander
27. indictments	**28.** unfavorable
29. Misfortunes	**30.** starvation
31. hesitates	**32.** relived

Section 4 Questions 31-34
Complete the Notes below
Write No More Than Two Words for each answer

In *The Penguin Lessons*, numerous penguins' carcasses are discovered. To get rid of the **31.**_____ is of vital concern.

Penguins' black and white patterns are served as the function of the **32.**_____ .

The thickness of penguin's **33.**_____ is 30 to 40 per square centimeter, almost triple than that of the flying birds.

Penguin's gland actually secretes the oil to make penguin's plumage **34.**_____ .

Questions 35-40

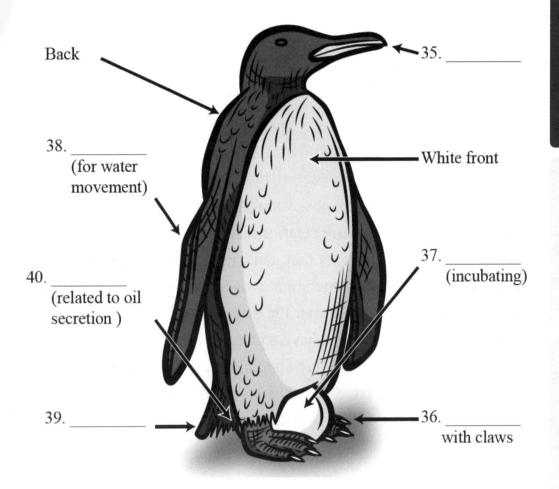

Back

35. _____

38. _____
(for water
movement)

White front

37. _____
(incubating)

40. _____
(related to oil
secretion)

39. _____

36. _____
with claws

影子跟讀練習 MP3 004

What is the benefit of possessing pets? Console when you are alone. Maintain a sustaining relationship by having a mutual topic. Film the adorable movements that generate many hits. Less annoying than raising kids. Great listeners that won't talk back. Be the spotlight whenever you walk them down the street. Be the matchmaker and attract other girls who want to have a picture with them. I've got to say these benefits all make our day special and more optimistic. Those gloomy emotions you have gathered at the office will soon die down when you hug the pet of yours. What does this have to do with today's topic.

擁有寵物的好處是什麼？當你孤獨時，安慰你。一段戀愛關係因為有共同話題而得以延續。拍攝可愛的動作以產生許多點閱。比起養小孩來說，寵物較不擾人。良好的聆聽者且不會回嘴。每當在街上溜寵物時，能成為矚目焦點。成為月老媒人，吸引其他想要跟寵物拍照的女孩們。我必須要說的是，這些好處都讓我們的每一天變得特別且更為樂觀。當你擁抱你的寵物時，那些在辦公室中你所積聚的憂鬱情緒都將消失殆盡。而這又與今天所談論的話題有什麼關係呢？

❶ console 安慰，撫慰

❷ sustain 維持，供養

❸ mutual 相互的，彼此的

❹ movement 動作；移動

❺ spotlight 聚光燈

❻ gloomy 陰鬱的；憂鬱的

The Penguin Lessons. It's about raising pets as well. And since "a thing is valued if it is rare", that's why I am choosing this topic instead of talking about dogs and cats that you have raised. It's kind of cool that the author has the penguin as a pet. Why? Most of the time, we can only see penguins in aquariums and zoos. The galvanizing tale will certainly make you delighted, and we are going to go over this book in a very quick manner.

《企鵝的課程》。這本書也是關於養寵物。而既然「物以稀為貴」，這就是為什麼我選了這個話題，而非討論你們所飼養的貓貓狗狗。作者有企鵝這樣的寵物有點酷酷的。為什麼呢？多數時候，我們僅能在水族館和動物園中看到企鵝。振奮人心的故事確實會讓你感到興高采烈，而我們會以飛快的速度看完這本書。

Let's skip those descriptions about the scenery and the comparison between fish and gulls. The beautiful day at the beach, but the scarcity of the number of penguins seems to tell us the warning that something is going on. It soon transpires that the conjecture is entirely correct. What the author has witnessed is not near the ecological collapse, but a catastrophe. More and more penguins are found dead on the shore, and they are obviously suffered from suffocation of oil and tar. What is desperately needed is to remove the oil slick. Ultimately, there is a penguin that still shows the sign of life. This has led to the serendipitous encounter between the two.

　　讓我們跳過那些關於風景和魚與海鷗對比的描述。海灘上景色宜人，但是企鵝數量的稀少似乎向我們傳達一種警告，有事情發生了。稍後證實了，這樣的猜測是完全正確的。作者所目睹的不是生態崩毀，而是個災難。在海岸上，出現了越來越多的企鵝屍體，企鵝顯然因為油和瀝青受到了窒息。迫切需要的是將水面上的浮油移除。最後，有隻企鵝仍有著生命跡象。這也促成了人和企鵝兩者的奇緣。

- ❶ aquarium 水族館
- ❷ galvanizing 振奮人心的
- ❸ scenery 風景，景色
- ❹ gull 鷗，海鷗
- ❺ transpire 結果證實
- ❻ conjecture 推測，猜測
- ❼ ecological 生態（學）的
- ❽ catastrophe 大災難
- ❾ suffocation 窒息；悶死
- ❿ serendipitous 機緣湊巧的；意外的

He takes the 10-pound penguin back to the apartment and has the shower for it, though this might not be good for the penguin in the long run. He wrote, "If my arm were to tire and that vicious beak came within striking distance." That is what we will be focusing on, the beak, the anatomy of penguins, so I am going the leave the rest of the story for you to read during your free time, and hand in the report next Friday.

作者把 10 磅重的企鵝帶回公寓中，並為其淋浴，儘管此舉對企鵝最終可能並非有助益。作者寫到「假如我的胳臂筋疲力盡，近在咫尺的企鵝惡喙就會招呼過來。」這也會是我們所關注的部分，企鵝的鳥嘴，企鵝的解剖構造，所以我會將書中剩餘的故事讓你們在空閒的時間去完成閱讀，並於下週五的時候遞交報告。

In Zoology, we have mentioned about the function of a black and white pattern, as can be seen in zebras and certain insects. Penguins' black and white patterns are served as the function of the **camouflage**. Their back exhibits black colors, whereas their front shows white hues, making predators confused and hard to distinguish.

在動物學，我們已經提過了關於黑白相間型態的功用，如同在斑馬或特定昆蟲上頭所見。企鵝的黑白型態也能充當成偽裝的功用。他們的背部顯示出了黑色，而他們身體前方展示出白的色澤，讓掠食者感到困惑，難以辨別。

On land, they walk with short steps clumsily, quite contrary to their swift movements in the water. They do have the ability to jump while using both legs. What about their eyesight? Their vision is considered poor when they are on land, but while they are in the water, it is a completely different story. To endure the coldness of ocean temperatures, penguin's feathers are massive that help them conserve energy and keep warm. The thickness of penguin's plumage is 30 to 40 per square centimeter, almost triple than that of the flying birds.

在陸地上，企鵝以短小的步伐行走，與牠們在水中的移動是大相逕庭的。企鵝也能夠用雙腿進行跳躍。那麼，企鵝的視力呢？企鵝的視力在陸地上時是被認為是不良的，但是當牠們在水中，這又是另一個全然不同的故事了。為了忍受海洋溫度的寒冷，企鵝厚大的羽毛幫助牠們儲存足夠的能量並保持溫暖。企鵝羽毛的厚度是每平方公分 30-40，幾乎是其他飛行鳥類的三倍多。

❶ apartment 公寓房間
❷ vicious 邪惡的；墮落的
❸ beak 鳥嘴
❹ anatomy 解剖結構
❺ camouflage 偽裝；掩飾
❻ hue 顏色，色彩
❼ clumsily 笨拙地；粗陋地
❽ eyesight 視力，目力
❾ massive 大而重的，厚實的
❿ conserve 保存；保護；節省

The size of their **bill** may be varied in accordance with the species. It will influence their consumption of food. Penguins which consume squid, fish and crustaceans exhibit long and thin bills, whereas those which eat krill demonstrate the bills that are shorter and wider.

企鵝的喙會根據種類而不同。這會影響到牠們攝食。以烏賊、魚類和甲殼綱動物為主食的企鵝，會演化出長且薄的喙，而那些以磷蝦為食者會顯示出較短且較寬的喙。

Penguins have **webbed feet** with visible claws, and since their feet can ensure the constancy of body temperatures, **the egg** of the penguin will be put between the feet for the incubation to happen, and heat loss is less likely to happen. Parents do have to keep a watchful eye for their babies.

企鵝的蹼足有清晰可見的爪子，而既然牠們的腳可以確保體溫的恆定，企鵝的蛋會被放置在兩腳之間，等待蛋的孵化，還有熱能的流失較不可能會發生。企鵝父母對於自己的小孩必須警惕地看著。

Penguins do have flippers. The function of the **flipper** is similar to that of birds' wings. They assist their water movements. As for **the tail**, it has multiple functions, and its use has been downplayed by many. However, in walking, climbing, sitting, and swimming, tails play an important role.

企鵝也有鰭足。鰭足的功用就近似於鳥類的翅膀。鰭足協助企鵝在水中的移動。至於尾巴的話，它有許多功用，而且其用處被許多人低估了。然而，在行走、攀爬、坐著和游泳，尾巴都扮演著重要的角色。

Lastly, I want to mention about the **gland** that is adjacent to the tail of the penguins. The gland actually secretes the oil to make penguin's plumage waterproof. And in the book, the author's kindness of washing away the body of the penguin makes it lose the ability of resistance to water. So tragically, it cannot swim back to the ocean...

　　最後，我想要提到的是關於鄰近企鵝尾巴部分的腺體。腺體實際上分泌了油脂，讓企鵝的羽毛能夠防水。而在書中，作者好心洗淨企鵝的身體，卻反而幫倒忙，讓企鵝失去了對水的抗性。所以，很悲劇地，企鵝無法游回海中...。

❶ consume 消耗，花費；耗盡
❷ squid 烏賊
❸ crustacean 甲殼綱動物
❹ webbed feet 蹼足
❺ constancy 恆久不變
❻ incubation 孵卵；熟慮
❼ watchful 警惕的；戒備的
❽ flipper 鰭足
❾ gland 腺體
❿ waterproof 防水的

試題解析

● **第 31 題**，*In The Penguin Lessons*, numerous penguins' carcasses are discovered. To get rid of the **31.＿＿＿＿＿** is of vital concern，對應到 More and more penguins are found dead on the shore, and they are obviously suffered from suffocation of oil and tar. What is desperately needed is to remove the oil slick，這題有進行改寫，remove 可以對應到 get rid of，What is desperately needed 可以對應到 is of vital concern，故答案為 **oil slick**。

● **第 32 題**，Penguins' black and white patterns are served as the function of the **32.＿＿＿＿＿**，對應到 In Zoology, we have mentioned about the function of a black and white pattern, as can be seen in zebras and certain insects. Penguins' black and white patterns are served as the function of the camouflage，試題與聽力訊息完全一致，並未改寫，定位到聽力訊息就能答對，故答案為 **camouflage**。

● **第 33 題**，The thickness of penguin's **33.＿＿＿＿＿** is 30 to 40 per square centimeter, almost triple than that of the flying birds.，對應到 The thickness of penguin's plumage is 30 to 40 per square centimeter, almost triple than that of the flying birds，試題與聽力訊息完全一致，並未改寫，定位到聽力訊息就能答對，故答案為 **plumage**。

- **第 34 題**，Penguin's gland actually secretes the oil to make penguin's plumage **34.**＿＿＿＿＿＿，對應到 The gland actually secretes the oil to make penguin's plumage waterproof，試題與聽力訊息完全一致，並未改寫，定位到聽力訊息就能答對，但需要耐心聽到聽力結尾，故答案為 **waterproof**。

- **第 35 題**，觀看圖表並對應到 The size of their **bill** may be varied in accordance with the species. It will influence their consumption of food，故答案為 **bill**。

- **第 36 題**，觀看圖表並對應到 Penguins have **webbed feet** with visible claws, and since their feet can ensure the constancy of body temperatures, **the egg** of the penguin will be put between the feet for the incubation to happen, and heat loss is less likely to happen，故答案為 **webbed feet**。圖表中多加了提示字，with claws，有降低難度跟協助定位。

- **第 37 題**，觀看圖表並對應到 Penguins have **webbed feet** with visible claws, and since their feet can ensure the constancy of body temperatures, **the egg** of the penguin will be put between the feet for the incubation to happen, and heat loss is less likely to happen，故答案為 **the egg**。圖表中多加了提示字，incubating，有降低難度跟協助定位。

- **第 38 題**，觀看圖表並對應到 Penguins do have flippers. The function of the **flipper** is similar to that of birds' wings，故答案為 **flipper**。圖表中多加了提示字，for water movement，有降低難度跟協助定位。

- **第 39 題**，觀看圖表並對應到 They assist their water movements. As for **the tail**, it has multiple functions, and its use has been downplayed by many，故答案為 **the tail**。

- **第 40 題**，觀看圖表並對應到 Lastly, I want to mention about the **gland** that is adjacent to the tail of the penguins，故答案為 **gland**。圖表中多加了提示字，related to oil secretion，有降低難度跟協助定位。

| Instruction | MP3 004

現在請再聽一次音檔，並做下列的測驗，檢視自己能否完成此填空測驗和強化自己聽力能力和拼字能力，降低並修正自己漏聽到聽力訊息的機會，大幅提升應考實力。

What is the benefit of possessing **1.**＿＿＿＿＿＿＿? Console when you are alone. Maintain a sustaining relationship by having a mutual topic. Film the **2.**＿＿＿＿＿＿ movements that generate many hits. Less annoying than raising kids. Great listeners that won't talk back. Be the **3.**＿＿＿＿＿＿ whenever you walk them down the street. Be the **4.**＿＿＿＿＿＿ and attract other girls who want to have a picture with them. I've got to say these benefits all make our day special and more **5.**＿＿＿＿＿＿. Those gloomy **6.**＿＿＿＿＿＿ you have gathered at the office will soon die down when you hug the pet of yours.

The Penguin Lessons. It's about raising pets as well. And since "a thing is valued if it is **7.**＿＿＿＿＿＿", that's why I am choosing this topic instead of talking about dogs and cats that you have raised. It's kind of cool that the author has the penguin as a pet. Why? Most of the time, we can only see penguins in **8.**＿＿＿＿＿＿ and zoos. The **9.**＿＿＿＿＿＿ tale will certainly make you delighted, and we are going to go over this book in a very quick manner.

Let's skip those descriptions about the **10.**＿＿＿＿＿＿ and the comparison between fish and gulls. The beautiful day at the beach, but the **11.**＿＿＿＿＿ of the number of penguins seems to tell us the warning that something is going on. It soon **12.**＿＿＿＿ that the conjecture is entirely correct. What the author has witnessed is not near the **13.**＿＿＿＿ collapse, but a **14.**＿＿＿＿＿. More and more penguins are found dead on the shore, and they are obviously suffered from **15.**＿＿＿＿ of oil and tar. What is desperately needed is to remove the oil slick. Ultimately, there is a penguin that still shows the sign of life. This has led to the **16.**＿＿＿＿ encounter between the two.

He takes the 10-pound penguin back to the **17.**＿＿＿＿＿ and has the shower for it, though this might not be good for the penguin in the long run. He wrote, "If my arm were to tire and that **18.**＿＿＿＿ beak came within striking distance."

In Zoology, we have mentioned about the **19.**＿＿＿＿ of a black and white pattern, as can be seen in **20.**＿＿＿＿ and certain **21.**＿＿＿＿. Penguins' black and white patterns are served as the function of the camouflage. Their back exhibits **22.**＿＿＿＿ colors, whereas their front shows white **23.**＿＿＿＿, making predators confused and hard to distinguish.

On land, they walk with short steps **24.**＿＿＿＿, quite contrary to their swift movements in the water. They do have the ability to jump while using both legs. What about their **25.**＿＿＿ ? Their vision is considered poor when they are on land, but while they are in the water, it is a completely different story. To endure the coldness of **26.**_____ temperatures, penguin's feathers are massive that help them **27.**_____ energy and keep warm. The thickness of penguin's **28.**_____ is 30 to 40 per square centimeter, almost triple than that of the flying birds.

The size of their bill may be varied in accordance with the species. It will influence their **29.**_____ of food. Penguins which consume squid, **30.**_____ and crustaceans exhibit long and thin bills, whereas those which eat krill demonstrate the bills that are shorter and wider.

Penguins have webbed feet with visible claws, and since their feet can ensure the **31.**_____ of body temperatures, the egg of the penguin will be put between the feet for the **32.**_____ to happen, and heat loss is less likely to happen. Parents do have to keep a watchful eye for their babies.

Penguins do have flippers. The function of the flipper is similar to that of birds' wings. They assist their **33.**_____ movements. As for the tail, it has multiple functions, and its use has been downplayed by many. However, in walking, climbing, sitting, and swimming, tails play an important role.

Lastly, I want to mention about the gland that is adjacent to the tail of the penguins. The gland actually secretes the oil to make penguin's plumage **34.**_____. And in the book, the author's kindness of washing away the body of the penguin makes it lose the ability of resistance to water. So tragically, it cannot swim back to the ocean...

| 參考答案 |

1. pets
2. adorable
3. spotlight
4. matchmaker
5. optimistic
6. emotions
7. rare
8. aquariums
9. galvanizing
10. scenery
11. scarcity
12. transpires
13. ecological
14. catastrophe
15. suffocation
16. serendipitous
17. apartment
18. vicious
19. function
20. zebras
21. insects
22. black
23. hues
24. clumsily
25. eyesight
26. ocean
27. conserve
28. plumage
29. consumption
30. fish
31. constancy
32. incubation
33. water
34. waterproof

Section 1 Questions 1-10

Complete the Notes below

Write No More than 2 Words for each answer

Noise ❶: roaring of **1.**_____.

Noise ❷:

● the movement of **2.**_____.

● and it turns out to be scorpions trying to look for a **3.**_____.

● They are evacuating because of the presence of the **4.**_____.

Noise ❸:

there's even a **5.**_____...

Snake and its trace:

- Underneath the blanket: the **6.**_____ .
- The trace of the snake: first, under the blanket
- and then eventually crawling towards the last ladder of the **7.**_____ .
- a torch or a **8.**_____ might be the help, if not, **9.**_____ would be just fine.

Milk tea

- good for the sleep

Excuse they came up with:

- the intrusion of a purple butterfly
- if it's the poisonous bee: light up the **10.**_____ .

- 第 1 題，roaring of 1.＿＿＿＿＿＿＿＿，對應到 roaring of **sandstorms**...it's best that we don't open the shaky window，聽力訊息和試題完全一致，故答案為 **sandstorms**。

- 第 2 題，the movement of 2.＿＿＿＿＿＿＿＿，對應到 perhaps about to...the sound of **insects** moving on these large pillars，moving 對應到 movement，還是一樣是昆蟲在柱子上移動，故答案為 **insects**。

- 第 3 題，it turns out to be scorpions trying to look for a 3.＿＿＿＿＿＿，對應到 I'm afraid that they are...trying to find a **shelter** here，句子有部分改寫，但都是指在找庇護所，故答案為 **shelter**。

- 第 4 題，They are evacuating because of the presence of the 4.＿＿＿＿＿＿＿，對應到 oh...because of the **rattlesnake**，句子有部分改寫，但都是指響尾蛇，故答案為 **rattlesnake**。

- 第 5 題，there's even a 5.＿＿＿＿＿＿＿...，對應到 oh there's even a **thunderstorm**...，聽力訊息和試題完全一致，故答案為 **thunderstorm**。

● 第 6 題，Underneath the blanket: the **6.**＿＿＿＿＿＿＿，對應到 oh my god, it's the **underpass**，聽力訊息有先提到響尾蛇爬到毯子下，而毯子下有密道，故答案為 **underpass**。

● 第 7 題，eventually crawling towards the last ladder of the **7.**＿＿ ＿＿＿＿＿＿，對應到 the snake is...crawling towards the last ladder of the **tunnel**，聽力訊息和試題完全一致，故答案為 **tunnel**。

● 第 8 題，a torch or a **8.**＿＿＿＿＿＿ might be the help，對應到 I don't know...do you have a torch or a **flashlight**，聽力訊息和試題完全一致，故答案為 **flashlight**。

● 第 9 題，if not, **9.**＿＿＿＿＿＿ would be just fine，對應到 I don't...but I think the **smartphone** would be ok...，聽力訊息和試題完全一致，故答案為 **smartphone**。

● 第 10 題，if it's the poisonous bee: light up the **10.**＿＿＿＿＿＿，對應到 there is a purple butterfly, intruding in...thank god it's not the poisonous bee...otherwise, I will have to light up the **scented candle**，都是指遇到有毒蜜蜂的話點燃有香氣的蠟燭，故答案為 **scented candle**。

影子跟讀練習 MP3 005

做完題目後，除了對答案知道錯的部分在哪外，更重要的是要修正自己聽力根本的問題，即聽力理解力和聽力專注力，聽力專注力的修正能逐步強化本身的聽力實力，所以現在請根據聽力內容「逐個段落」、「數個段落」或「整篇」進行跟讀練習，提升在實際考場時專注聽完每個訊息、定位出關鍵考點和搭配筆記回答完所有題目。Go!

| B |

thanks again for the meal...quite delicious

| B |

再次要謝謝所提供的餐點...相當美味

| A |

Good night...and don't go out without informing any one of us here...

| A |

晚安...還有別在未告知的情況下跑到外頭喔！...

| B |

thanks for the notification...

| B |

謝謝告知...

| B |

Wow, what's that noise?

| B |

哇！那是什麼聲音啊？

| C |

wind...roaring of **sandstorms**...it's best that we don't open the shaky window.

| C |

風...沙塵暴的呼嘯聲...我們最好別打開那搖搖欲墜的窗戶吧！

| B |

thank God...it's not raining...what's that noise?

| B |

謝天謝地...沒下雨...那是什麼聲音啊？

| C |

perhaps about to...the sound of **insects** moving on these large pillars

| C |

可能正要下雨了...這些大柱子上頭都有昆蟲移動的聲音

| B |

don't tell me those are scorpions...

| B |

別告訴我那是毒蠍...

| C |

I'm afraid that they are...trying to find a **shelter** here...as long as we keep calm and remain immovable.

| C |

恐怕要跟你說...就是毒蠍啊！...試圖在這裡尋求庇護所...只要我們保持冷靜且維持不動就好了啊！

| B |

there's got to be something that we can do

| B |

一定有什麼我們可以採取的行動

| C |

I think they are retreating for reason not yet fully understood...

| C |

我想他們正因無法完全理解的原因在撤退中...

| B |

oh...because of the **rattlesnake**? Kind of cute...

| B |

噢！...因為那條響尾蛇嗎？...有點可愛...

| C |

perhaps it comes here to rescue us because we didn't order it for dinner...

| C |

或許那條響尾蛇來這裡救我們，因為我們剛才晚餐沒點蛇羹...

| B |

oh there's even a **thunderstorm**...I do hope the thunderbolt won't tear the roof...

| B |

噢！...甚至下起大雷雨了呢！...我還真的希望雷擊不會把屋頂拆了...

| C |

where is the trace of the snake? Not on the pillar anymore...

| C |

蛇跑去哪裡了呢？不在柱子上頭了...

| B |

I think it is under the blanket...

| B |

我想牠鑽進毯子底下了...

| C |

what's underneath?

| C |

毯子下面是什麼啊？

| B |

oh my god, it's the **underpass**？

| B |

我的天啊！是條地下通道。

| C |

and the snake is...crawling towards the last ladder of the **tunnel**

| C |

而這條蛇正...朝著通道最後一個階梯爬去。

| B |

is it the larder of the snake?

| B |

會是蛇的巢穴嗎？

| C |

I don't know...do you have a torch or a **flashlight**? You always have the flashlight when traveling...

| C |

我不知道...你有火把或者是手電筒嗎？旅行時，你總會攜帶手電筒的...

| B |

I don't...but I think the **smartphone** would be ok...using yours or mine...can you check the battery...

| B |

我沒帶唉！...但是我想手機也可以吧...用你的還是我的手機啊！...你可以檢查一下電力嗎...？

| C |

90%...perhaps enough for us to do the adventure...but there is no signal...

| C |

還有 90% 電力...或許夠我們來趟冒險...但是這裡完全沒訊號...

| B |

what else do we have to carry...with us when we go down...do we have to wait until the other two come back to the room...oh someone is knocking on the door...

| B |

當我們往下走的時候，我們還會需要攜帶些什麼啊！...我們還要等到兩個隊友回到這間房間吧！...噢！有人在敲房間門...

| A |

Do you guys need some milk tea? It's good for the sleep.

| A |

你們會需要些奶茶嗎？對睡眠有幫助喔！

| B |

we are not thirsty...thanks...

| B |

我們不渴...多謝了。

| A |

Are you guys ok? The voice seems trembling...

| A |

你們還好嗎？聲音聽起來有些發抖...

| B |

sure...while we are trying to appreciate the beautiful vase on the table, there is a purple butterfly, intruding in...thank god it's not the poisonous bee...otherwise, I will have to light up the **scented candle**.

| B |

當然囉...只是我們正在欣賞桌上的漂亮花瓶時，有隻紫色的蝴蝶突然闖入...謝天謝地，還好不是隻有毒的蜜蜂，否則我就要點燃有香味的蠟燭了

| A |

whatever you do, please don't open the vase...

| A |

不論你們做什麼，都別打開花瓶喔...

| Instruction | MP3 005

現在請再聽一次音檔，並做下列的測驗，檢視自己能否完成此填空測驗和強化自己聽力能力和拼字能力，降低並修正自己漏聽到聽力訊息的機會，大幅提升應考實力。

| B |

thanks again for the **1.**_____...quite delicious

| A |

Good **2.**_____...and don't go out without informing any one of us here...

| B |

thanks for the **3.**_____...

| B |

Wow, what's that noise?

| C |

wind...roaring of **4.**_____...it's best that we don't open the shaky **5.**_____.

| B |

thank God...it's not raining...what's that **6.**_____?

| C |

perhaps about to...the sound of **7.**_____ moving on these large pillars

| B |

don't tell me those are **8.**_____ ...

| C |

I'm afraid that they are...trying to find a **9.**_____ here...as long as we keep **10.**_____ and remain **11.**_____ .

| B |

there's got to be something that we can do

| C |

I think they are **12.**_____ for reason not yet fully understood...

| B |

oh...because of the **13.**_____? Kind of cute...

| C |

perhaps it comes here to rescue us because we didn't order it for **14.**_____ ...

| B |

oh there's even a thunderstorm...I do hope the **15.**_____ won't tear the roof...

| C |

where is the trace of the snake? Not on the **16.**_____
anymore...

| B |

I think it is under the **17.**_____ ...

| C |

what's underneath?

| B |

oh my god, it's the **18.**_____ ?

| C |

and the snake is...crawling towards the last ladder of the **19.**_____
_____

| B |

is it the larder of the snake?

| C |

I don't know...do you have a **20.**_____ or a flashlight? You
always have the flashlight when traveling...

| B |

I don't...but I think the **21.**_____ would be ok...using yours
or mine...can you check the **22.**_____ ...

| C |

90%...perhaps enough for us to do the adventure...but there is no **23.**_____...

| B |

what else do we have to carry...with us when we go down...do we have to wait until the other two come back to the room...oh someone is knocking on the **24.**_____...

| A |

Do you guys need some **25.**_____? It's good for the sleep.

| B |

we are not thirsty...thanks...

| A |

Are you guys ok? The voice seems **26.**_____...

| B |

sure...while we are trying to appreciate the beautiful vase on the table, there is a **27.**_____ butterfly, intruding in...thank god it's not the **28.**_____ bee...otherwise, I will have to light up the scented **29.**_____.

| A |

whatever you do, please don't open the **30.**_____...

1. meal
2. night
3. notification
4. sandstorms
5. window
6. noise
7. insects
8. scorpions
9. shelter
10. calm
11. immovable
12. retreating
13. rattlesnake
14. dinner
15. thunderbolt
16. pillar
17. blanket
18. underpass
19. tunnel
20. torch
21. smartphone
22. battery
23. signal
24. door
25. milk tea
26. trembling
27. purple
28. poisonous
29. candle
30. vase

Section 2
Questions 11-20

Complete the tables below. Write **NO more than two words** for each answer

Three Classics	
The History of Tom Jones, a Founding	● Still parents should be **11.** _____ .
Gone with the Wind	● Love is blind to the person who is in love, so **12.** _____ like your parents can be of great help.
	● Moreover, one's youth is fleeting. You certainly cannot turn back time to your twentysomething years. One's **13.** _____ in love dwindles as you age.
	● Going after a guy who only wants to be your friend is the **14.** _____ in the relationship.
	● Ashely's family cherishes a lot of things, like books, poetry, **15.** _____ , and music. ● Fourth, don't try to change a man.

Gone with the Wind	• Changing a man's **16.**_____ in marriage is considered ridiculous even with one's outer beauty.
Middlemarch	• Mr. Brooke, Dorothea's uncle adopts a **17.**_____ approach to children's marriage.
	• It soon transpires that Dorothea won't get the **18.**_____ from Casaubon.
	• Dorothea's feelings as a woman need to be understood, but her husband has shown little interest in her viewpoints. Will, on the other hand, can always find her viewpoints **19.**_____.
	• Not to mention, Dorothea and Casaubon's honeymoon at Rome is a **20.**_____.

影子跟讀練習 MP3 006

做完題目後，除了對答案知道錯的部分在哪外，更重要的是要修正自己聽力根本的問題，即聽力理解力和聽力專注力，聽力專注力的修正能逐步強化本身的聽力實力，所以現在請根據聽力內容「逐個段落」、「數個段落」或「整篇」進行跟讀練習，提升在實際考場時專注聽完每個訊息、定位出關鍵考點和搭配筆記回答完所有題目。Go!

Do parents have the right the meddle their children's marriage? Let's take a look at what the author has to say in *The History of Tom Jones, a Founding*, please flip the page to book 14 chapter 8.

父母有權干涉小孩的婚姻嗎？讓我們看一下作者對於此議題有甚麼看法，請翻至第 14 卷第 8 章。

"I have therefore always thought it unreasonable in parents to desire to chuse for their children on this occasion." "It is, however, true that, though a parent will not, I think, wisely prescribe, he ought to be **consulted** on this occasion; and in strictness, perhaps, should at least have a negative voice."

「所以我總是在想，父母幫子女選擇結婚對象一點都不合理。」「然而，雖然明智的父母確實不該獨斷專行，但婚姻大事最好還是詢問一下父母的意見。或許，嚴格來說，應該至少有反面的聲音。」

I think these statements say it all, but still they appear to be not that convincing to some people. So we have to look at another classics,

Gone with the Wind, to see why children should take parents viewpoints into account.

我想這些陳述就説明一切了，但是對於有些人來説，這些論點仍不是那麼有説服力。所以我們要看一下另一本經典作品《亂世佳人》看看小孩是否該把父母的觀點列入考量。

❶ meddle 干涉；管閒事
❷ marriage 結婚，婚姻
❸ unreasonable 不講理的，非理智的
❹ strictness 嚴格；嚴謹
❺ convincing 有説服力的；令人信服的
❻ viewpoint 視角；觀點

Parents have lived longer than their kids, so it is reasonable to say that they can see through the person that you are dating. Love is blind to the person who is in love, so **bystanders** like your parents can be of great help, and you won't take a meandering route to realize certain truth. Furthermore, your youth is fleeting. You certainly cannot turn back time to your twentysomething years. One's market value in love wanes as you age.

父母活得比他們的孩子都久，所以可以合理地去推論出，他們能看穿你正在交往的對象。戀愛中的人是盲目的，所以像你父母這樣的旁觀者就能有很大的幫助，而且你不會走曲折的路才意識到某些真理。此外，你的青春是短暫的。你確實不可能讓時光倒回至你 20 多歲的時候。在戀愛中，一個人的市場價值會隨著你的老去而變得不值。

In *Gone with the Wind*, at the very beginning of the novel, Scarlett's father, Gerald has foreseen Ashley is not the fit for Scarlett. At first, he says, "the best marriages are when the parents choose for the girl." Second, he points out the big mistake that Scarlett is trying to make. She has been running after a man that doesn't love her. It's the **taboo** in the relationship. Thirdly, he analyzes how different Ashely's family is to their own. Their family value a lot in things, like books, poetry, **oil paintings**, and music. Fourth, don't try to change a man. No wives in the world are able to change the **personality** of a man in marriage, and Scarlett is innocent enough to believe that with her beauty, she can totally do that. It's too absurd.

在《亂世佳人》，小說非常前面的地方，思嘉麗的父親，傑拉爾德早已預見艾希禮不適合思嘉麗。起初，他說道「最美滿的婚姻就是那些父母做主為女兒選擇的婚姻了。」第二，他指出思嘉麗正要犯下一個大錯。她一直在追求一個不愛她的男人。這是戀愛關係中的大忌。第三，他分析了艾希禮家裡跟他們家族的差異處。艾希禮家族重視很多東西，像是書籍、詩歌、油畫和音樂。第四，不要試圖去改變一個男人。世界上，沒有一個妻子能夠在一段婚姻關係中去改變一個男人的性格，而思嘉麗天真到相信，以她的美貌，她絕對能夠做到改變男人這點。這太荒謬了。

Her father has mentioned lots of important things in adult relationships. One thing I do want to point out is the lack of understanding about oneself. Scarlett doesn't know herself at all. That's why at the very end of the fiction. She confesses that she doesn't love Ashley. She doesn't need the time of three marriages to realize that. She is obviously the type that parents shouldn't interfere with her affection, and she will go whatever she wants.

　　她父親已經提到許多在成人戀愛關係中的重要事情。有件我想要指出的事情是，對自己本身不夠了解。思嘉麗一點也不了解她自己。那也就是為什麼在小說的結尾。她坦承，她不愛艾希禮。她不需要三段婚姻去意識到這點。她顯然是個父母不該干涉她戀情的類型，而且她還是會追尋她自己所想要的。

❶ bystander 旁觀者

❷ meander 迂迴曲折

❸ wane（月）虧，缺

❹ foresee 預見；預知

❺ taboo 禁忌，忌諱

❻ innocent 無罪的，清白的

❼ confess 坦白，供認

❽ obviously 明顯地；顯然地

❾ interfere 介入；干涉

❿ affection 情愛

In *Middlemarch*, we have to look at Dorothea's marriage. Mr. Brooke, Dorothea's uncle is so unlike Gerald in *Gone with the Wind*. He adopts a liberal approach to children's marriage. "You shall do as you like." "as pretending to be wise for young people - no uncle could pretend to judge what sort of marriage would turn out well for a young girl." Furthermore, Dorothea's decided that one of the pursuers, Casaubon is the perfect fit for her.

　　在《米德爾鎮的春天》裡，我們要看的是關於多羅西亞的婚姻。布魯克，也就是多羅西亞的伯父，跟在《亂世佳人》的傑拉爾德是非常南轅北轍。布魯克對於小孩的婚姻採取了開明的手法。「妳想選誰就選誰。」「至於扮演智者教導年輕人這種事。世界上沒有哪個伯父可以自以為地斷言，哪一種婚姻比較幸福。」此外，多羅西亞已經決定了其中一位追求者卡索邦對她來說就是完美的對象。

What is the result of Dorothea's marriage? In chapter 37, Dorothea realizes that Casaubon doesn't seem the one for her. She doesn't get the **guidance** from Casaubon as she expected. Casaubon exhibits little interest in what Dorothea has to say, ignoring Dorothea as a woman, has the need to be understood. Will, on the other hand, can always find her viewpoints refreshing. Not to mention, Dorothea and Casaubon's honeymoon at Rome is a **fiasco**. Disagreement in opinions seems to mark a bad ending for their marriage. Casaubon is Dorothea's choice of a man, putting her at a better advantage than most women, but their personalities and conflicts in several things are the downside for a marriage to sustain...

多羅西亞的婚姻結果又是如何呢？在第 37 章，她意識到卡索邦似乎不是她的真命天子。她無法如期的得到卡索邦的指導。卡索邦對於多羅西亞所表達的看法顯得興趣缺缺，忽略了多羅西亞是個女人，也有被了解的需求。威爾，相反地，總能在多羅西亞的觀點中找出新意。更別提，多羅西亞和卡索邦在羅馬的蜜月旅行是個大災難。意見不合似乎標誌著他們婚姻會有個壞結局。卡索邦是多羅西亞自己選的男人，讓她比大多數女性都已經更具優勢了，但是兩人之間的個性和幾件事情的衝突對於維繫一段婚姻是個缺點...

（註：卡索邦經濟富裕。對於當時能嫁到這麼有錢的男人，多羅西亞真的算是比很多女性幸運，而且在卡索邦死後，更留了房產和一大筆錢。多羅

西亞也不是因為男方經濟條件優渥才選擇他。）

To sum up, we have talked two approaches, and it is up for you to figure out should parents offer suggestions to kids when they are about to get married?

總之，我們已經談論兩個方法了，要由你去理出，當小孩要結婚時，父母是否應該要提出建議？

❶ liberal 開明的，公允的

❷ pretend 佯裝；假裝

❸ pursuer 追求者

❹ guidance 指導；引導

❺ expect 預期；期待

❻ interest 興趣；關注

❼ refreshing 使人耳目一新的

❽ fiasco 慘敗

❾ advantage 有利條件，優點

❿ downside 不利；下降趨勢

- **第 11 題**，Still parents should be **11.**_____，對應到 It is, however, true that, though a parent will not, I think, wisely prescribe, he ought to be consulted on this occasion，ought to be 換成了 should be，故答案為 **consulted**。

- **第 12 題**，Love is blind to the person who is in love, so **12.** _____ like your parents can be of great help，對應到 Love is blind to the person who is in love, so bystanders like your parents can be of great help, and you won't take a meandering route to realize certain truth，試題與聽力訊息完全一致並未改寫，故答案為 **bystanders**。

- **第 13 題**，Moreover, one's youth is fleeting. You certainly cannot turn back time to your twentysomething years. One's **13.**_____ in love dwindles as you age，對應到 You certainly cannot turn back time to your twentysomething years. One's market value in love wanes as you age，dwindle 換成了 wane，但其他訊息不變，故答案為 **market value**。

- **第 14 題**，Going after a guy who only wants to be your friend is the **14.**_____ in the relationship.，對應到 She has been running after a man that doesn't love her. It's the taboo in the relationship，has been running 換成了 going after，但其他訊息不變，故答案為 **taboo**。

● 第 15 題，Ashely's family cherishes a lot of things, like books, poetry, **15.**＿＿＿＿＿＿, and music.，對應到 Their family value a lot in things, like books, poetry, oil paintings, and music，values 換成了 cherishes，但其他訊息不變，故答案為 **oil paintings**。

● 第 16 題，Changing a man's **16.**＿＿＿＿＿＿ in marriage is considered ridiculous even with one's outer beauty，對應到 Fourth, don't try to change a man. No wives in the world are able to change the personality of a man in marriage, and Scarlett is innocent enough to believe that with her beauty，句子有改寫整併，還是可以馬上就定位到 change，故答案為 **personality**。

● 第 17 題，Mr. Brooke, Dorothea's uncle adopts a **17.**＿＿＿＿＿＿ approach to children's marriage，對應到 He adopts a liberal approach to children's marriage，試題與聽力訊息完全一致並未改寫，故答案為 **liberal**。

● 第 18 題，It soon transpires that Dorothea won't get the **18.**＿＿＿＿＿＿ from Casaubon，對應到 In chapter 37, Dorothea realizes that Casaubon doesn't seem the one for her. She doesn't get the guidance from Casaubon as she expected，the 後面仍是對應的名詞 guidance，故答案為 **guidance**。

- 第 19 題，Dorothea's feelings as a woman need to be understood, but her husband has shown little interest in her viewpoints. Will, on the other hand, can always find her viewpoints **19.**_____，對應到 Casaubon exhibits little interest in what Dorothea has to say, ignoring Dorothea as a woman, has the need to be understood. Will, on the other hand, can always find her viewpoints **refreshing**，試題與聽力訊息完全一致並未改寫，故答案為 **refreshing**。

- 第 20 題，Not to mention, Dorothea and Casaubon's honeymoon at Rome is a **20.**_____，對應到 Not to mention, Dorothea and Casaubon's honeymoon at Rome is a fiasco，試題與聽力訊息完全一致並未改寫，故答案為 **fiasco**。

▶▶ 填空測驗

| Instruction | 〔MP3 006〕

現在請再聽一次音檔，並做下列的測驗，檢視自己能否完成此填空測驗和強化自己聽力能力和拼字能力，降低並修正自己漏聽到聽力訊息的機會，大幅提升應考實力。

Do parents have the right to **1.**_____ their children's marriage? Let's take a look at what the author has to say in *The History of Tom Jones, a Founding*, please flip the page to book 14 chapter **8.**

"I have therefore always thought it unreasonable in parents to desire to chuse for their children on this occasion." "It is, however, true that, though a parent will not, I think, wisely prescribe, he ought to be **2.**_____ on this occasion; and in strictness, perhaps, should at least have a **3.**_____ voice."

I think these **4.**_____ say it all, but still they appear to be not that **5.**_____ to some people. So we have to look at another classics, *Gone with the Wind*, to see why children should take parents viewpoints into account.

Parents have lived longer than their **6.**_____, so it is reasonable to say that they can see through the person that you are dating. Love is blind to the person who is in love, so **7.**_____ like your parents can be of great help, and you won't take a meandering route to realize certain truth. Furthermore, your **8.**_____

_____ is fleeting. You certainly cannot turn back time to your twentysomething years. One's market value in love **9.**_____ as you age.

In *Gone with the Wind*, at the very beginning of the novel, Scarlett's father, Gerald has foreseen Ashley is not the **10.**_____ for Scarlett. At first, he says, "the best marriages are when the parents choose for the girl." Second, he points out the big mistake that Scarlett is trying to make. She has been running after a **11.**_____ that doesn't love her. It's the **12.**_____ in the relationship. Thirdly, he analyzes how different Ashely's family is to their own. Their family value a lot in things, like books, **13.**_____, oil paintings, and **14.**_____. Fourth, don't try to change a man. No wives in the world are able to change the personality of a man in marriage, and Scarlett is innocent enough to believe that with her **15.**_____, she can totally do that. It's too absurd.

Her father has mentioned lots of important things in adult **16.**_____. One thing I do want to point out is the lack of understanding about oneself. Scarlett doesn't know herself at all. That's why at the very end of the **17.**_____. She confesses that she doesn't love Ashley. She doesn't need the time of **18.**_____ marriages to realize that. She is obviously the type that parents shouldn't interfere with her **19.**_____, and she will go whatever she wants.

In *Middlemarch*, we have to look at Dorothea's marriage. Mr. Brooke, Dorothea's **20.**_____ is so unlike Gerald in *Gone with the*

Wind. He adopts a **21.**_____ approach to children's marriage. "You shall do as you like." "as pretending to be wise for young people - no uncle could pretend to judge what sort of marriage would turn out well for a young girl." Furthermore, Dorothea's decided that one of the **22.**_____, Casaubon is the perfect fit for her.

What is the result of Dorothea's marriage? In chapter 37, Dorothea realizes that Casaubon doesn't seem the one for her. She doesn't get the **23.**_____ from Casaubon as she expected. Casaubon exhibits little interest in what Dorothea has to say, ignoring Dorothea as a woman, has the need to be understood. Will, on the other hand, can always find her viewpoints **24.**_____. Not to mention, Dorothea and Casaubon's **25.**_____ at Rome is a fiasco. Disagreement in **26.**_____ seems to mark a bad ending for their marriage. Casaubon is Dorothea's choice of a man, putting her at a better **27.**_____ than most women, but their personalities and **28.**_____ in several things are the **29.**_____ for a marriage to sustain...

To sum up, we have talked two approaches, and it is up for you to figure out should parents offer **30.**_____ to kids when they are about to get married?

參考答案

1. meddle
2. consulted
3. negative
4. statements
5. convincing
6. kids
7. bystanders
8. youth
9. wanes
10. fit
11. man
12. taboo
13. poetry
14. music
15. beauty
16. relationships
17. fiction
18. three
19. affection
20. uncle
21. liberal
22. pursuers
23. guidance
24. refreshing
25. honeymoon
26. opinions
27. advantage
28. conflicts
29. downside
30. suggestions

Section 3
Questions 21-30

Complete the tables below. Write **NO more than two words** for each answer

definition	• To attract the attention of moviegoers and readers, the **21.**_____ of love is needed.
1984	• The lecturer feels empathic and sympathetic for the **22.**_____ who doesn't seem to know what love is.
	• He wants to direct his **23.**_____ by solely focusing on his work, but he totally can't.
	• It is the love that makes him **24.**_____ to live.
	• Eventually they have a meeting on a Sunday afternoon, but he has no **25.**_____ .

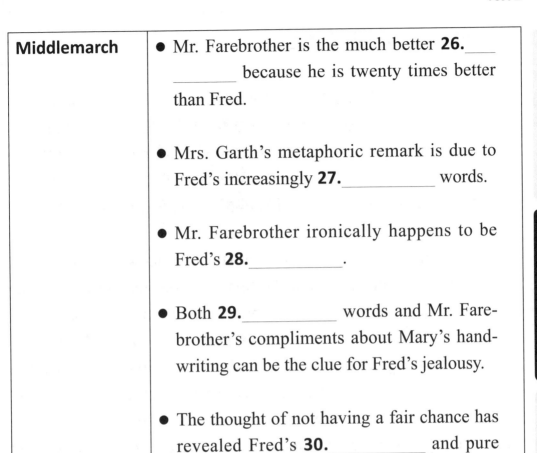

Middlemarch	• Mr. Farebrother is the much better **26.**___ _____ because he is twenty times better than Fred.
	• Mrs. Garth's metaphoric remark is due to Fred's increasingly **27.**_____ words.
	• Mr. Farebrother ironically happens to be Fred's **28.**_____.
	• Both **29.**_____ words and Mr. Farebrother's compliments about Mary's handwriting can be the clue for Fred's jealousy.
	• The thought of not having a fair chance has revealed Fred's **30.**_____ and pure love towards Mary.

Test 1

Test 2

Test 3

Test 4

影子跟讀練習 MP3 007

做完題目後，除了對答案知道錯的部分在哪外，更重要的是要修正自己聽力根本的問題，即聽力理解力和聽力專注力，聽力專注力的修正能逐步強化本身的聽力實力，所以現在請根據聽力內容「逐個段落」、「數個段落」或「整篇」進行跟讀練習，提升在實際考場時專注聽完每個訊息、定位出關鍵考點和搭配筆記回答完所有題目。Go!

What is it about the first love that still fascinates most of us? No matter what the outcome about the first love, our memories bring us back to pureness of the love. The innocence that makes it so special and memorable. Only the **pureness** of love can make people resonated. For a great movie or a fascinating fiction, it is actually a vital element, otherwise, it is just two great looking people getting loved. That won't attract the attention of moviegoers and readers. Let alone making any money. For today's class, we are going to talk about its virginity by using two great bestsellers, *1984* and *Middlemarch*.

對我們大多數的人來說，初戀是什麼，為何仍讓我們沉醉其中？不論我們初戀的結果為何，我們的記憶將我們帶至純潔的戀愛的時候。純潔無瑕讓戀愛變得如此特別且記憶猶新。只有純潔無瑕的戀愛能讓人們有所共鳴。對一個偉大的電影或者是另人著迷的小説，它確實是重要的要素；否則，僅僅是兩個極好看的人相戀。那無法吸引電影愛好者和讀者的注意力。更別說是要賺任何錢了。在今天的課堂中，我們會藉由《1984》和《米德爾鎮的春天》談論初戀的純潔。

In *1984*, Winston is the **protagonist** and eventually falls in love with another girl. The point is he is married. I'm not recommending you to be the other woman. But I feel kind of empathic and sympathetic for him. The person who doesn't seem to know what love is and eventually gets married. Some of us are like him, who doesn't know what love is. Then eventually have a date with someone, ending up getting together and after a few years...they get married and have kids...until one day, they realize they don't love each other. Winston is already 39 years old, so I feel bad for him to be so late to realize what love is...

在《1984》，溫斯頓是主角，而最終與另一位女子相戀。重點是他已經結婚了。我並不建議你去當第三者。但是對於溫斯頓我卻有著同理心和同情在。一個似乎不知道戀愛是什麼，而最終結了婚的人。我們當中也會有人像他一樣，不了解戀愛到底為何。然後，最終與一個人交往了，在一起，於幾年後...他們結了婚並有了小孩...直到有一天，他們意識到他們並不愛彼此。溫斯頓已經 39 歲了，所以對於他這麼晚才意識到什麼是戀愛這檔事...感到遭糕。

❶ fascinate 迷住，使神魂顛倒

❷ outcome 結果；結局

❸ innocence 天真無邪，純真

❹ memorable 值得懷念的；難忘的

❺ pureness 清潔；純粹

❻ protagonist 主演；主角

❼ recommend 推薦，介紹

❽ empathic 具同理心的

❾ sympathetic 同情的；有同情心的
❿ realize 意識到

When he comes to the realization that he is in love with the girl, he wants to see her again. He wants to shift the **attention** by solely focusing on his work, but he totally can't. It is this kind of love that makes him desired to live. He even has the thought of her young naked body. He has the crazy idea that the girl might change her mind or suddenly slip away from him...he feels tortured and sensitive...eventually they have a date on a Sunday afternoon...that marks a great beginning for him...

　　當他了解到他喜愛上那個女子時，他想要再見到她。他想要將注意力移到僅專注在自己的工作上頭，但是卻完全無法做到。就是這樣的戀愛讓他渴望能活著。他甚至想到她年輕赤裸的身體。他有了瘋狂的想法，就是那個女子可能會改變心意或是突然地從他身邊溜走...他變得敏感而且備受折磨...最終，他們在星期天下午有場約會...那替他標誌著很棒的開端...。

　　（註：在小説所設定的時空背景，在那種處處受監控等等的環境之下生活，活著似乎是受罪。）

What makes me feel great about the development is Winston's candidness.

"I'm thirty-nine years old. I've got a wife that I can't get rid of. I've got varicose veins. I've got five false teeth."

　　讓我覺得很棒的故事發展是關於溫斯頓的坦率。

「我三十九歲了，有一個甩不掉的老婆，腳上有靜脈性潰瘍，還有五顆假牙。」

The next moment, the kiss and touch and other details all make it so believable. Winston's not having **physical desire** also alludes to the fact that he is totally in love with the girl. It's the symbol of the pure love, a sharp contrast to things happening in an earlier chapter that Winston has sex with a woman who is 50 years old. He enters the room, and just does it...

下一刻，親吻和接觸以及其他細節都讓這個戀愛令人如此信服。溫斯頓沒有任何的身體慾望，這也間接指出了他完全愛上了這個女子。這是單純戀愛的象徵，與早先溫斯頓與一個年紀 50 歲的女子發生性關係的情節有極大的反差。對該女子，他進房間，然後就做了...。

❶ realization 領悟；認識
❷ shift 替換，更換；變動
❸ desire 渴望；要求
❹ thought 想法；見解 [C]
❺ torture 折磨；使為難
❻ sensitive 敏感的
❼ candidness 率直
❽ varicose 靜脈曲張的
❾ vein 靜脈，血管
❿ believable 可信的

In *Middlemarch*, we are going to talk about different aspect of the pure love. Some attributes such as jealousy are involved.

在《米德爾鎮的春天》，我們要談論的是關於純戀愛的不同面向。有些特質，例如忌妒，會列入探討項目中。

Love is not as simple as two people liking with each other. Other people, such as parents all play a key role, and in Fred's case, the greatest hindrance comes from Lucy. Lucy obviously wants her girl, Mary, to get married with someone with a great deal of fortune. Fred was born in a wealthy family, but Mr. Farebrother is twenty times better than Fred, making him the much better prospect. Mrs. Garth cannot say anything to her husband, and eventually can no longer endure Fred's increasingly **vexing** words. So she says "Yes, young people are usually blind to everything but their own wishes, and seldom imagine how much those wishes cost others." Bitter and hurtful remarks have led to Fred's sudden departure, and his jealousy towards Mr. Farebrother, who ironically happens to be his **envoy**.

戀愛並不只是兩個人彼此互相喜歡這樣簡單。其他人，例如父母也扮演了關鍵的角色，而在弗烈德的例子中，最大的阻礙來自露西。露西顯然希望他的女兒瑪莉嫁給有許多財富的人。弗烈德儘管出生於富有人家，但是菲爾布勒卻比弗烈德要好 20 倍，讓菲爾布勒成為了更好的對象。葛爾斯太太在面對自己丈夫不能說什麼，而最終無法再忍受弗烈德越來越惱人的言語。所以她說道「是啊！年輕人眼裡向來只有自己的願望，從來想像不到那些願望會造成別人多少損失。」挖苦和傷人的話語已經促使弗烈德突然的離席，而弗烈德忌妒菲爾布勒，而很諷刺的是其碰巧是弗烈德的請託人。

On his way to Lowick, we can clearly see Fred is obviously in love. Now his anxiety includes Mary's feelings towards him and Mr. Farebrother as a rival. His **satirizing** words towards Mrs. Farebrother and his sensitivity towards Mr. Farebrother's compliments about Mary's handwriting have demonstrated his jealousy.

在他回到洛威克的途中，我們可以清楚地看到弗烈德顯然戀愛了。現在他的憂慮包含了瑪莉對他的感覺，以及菲爾布勒這個情敵。他對菲爾布勒太太的諷刺字眼，以及他對於菲爾布勒稱讚瑪莉手寫字都顯示出了他的忌妒。

Mr. Farebrother is kind enough to let those two to have a space to talk to each other privately, but his thoughtfulness is mistaken by Fred.

菲爾布勒很好心的讓他們兩人有空間可以彼此私下談話，但是他的體貼卻受到弗烈德的誤解。

It's of no use, whatever I do, Mary, you are sure to marry Mr. Farebrother at last. Fred even thinks he doesn't have a fair chance...

「瑪莉不管我怎麼做都沒有用，妳最後一定會嫁給菲爾布勒先生。」弗烈德甚至認為他沒有公平競爭的機會...

Fred's words all show his **spontaneity** and pure love towards Mary...it soon transpires that Fred is thinking it in the wrong way. absurdly adorable. Fred is the one who proclaims his love towards Mary, and the fact that Mary is not in love with Mr. Farebrother making Fred feel relieved.

Test 1

Test 2

Test 3

Test 4

弗烈德的言語都顯示出了他對瑪莉的真情流露和單純的愛...最終證實了，弗烈德想錯了。極其可愛。弗烈德是位宣示自己對瑪莉的愛的人，瑪莉不愛菲爾布勒這點也讓弗烈德感到如釋重負。

And it is this pureness that makes Mary and Fred's part so refreshing and delightful. After all, readers want a heart-felt story. Fred's dorky charm is obviously one of them.

而也因為這個純潔的戀愛讓瑪莉和弗烈德的部分充滿新意和興奮。畢竟，讀者想要的是真切的故事。弗烈德傻呆魅力顯然就是其中之一...。

❶ attribute 特質
❷ hindrance 妨礙，障礙
❸ fortune 財產，財富
❹ wealthy 富裕的
❺ prospect 前景，前途
❻ vexing 使人厭煩的
❼ envoy 請託人
❽ satirizing 諷刺的
❾ thoughtfulness 體貼
❿ delightful 令人高興的

試題解析

● **第 21 題**，To attract the attention of moviegoers and readers, the **21.** of love is needed，對應到 Only the pureness of love can make people resonated. For a great movie or a fascinating fiction, it is actually a vital element, otherwise, it is just two great looking people getting loved. That won't attract the attention of moviegoers and readers，可以由對應到的訊息進行反推，而成為試題改寫後的 to attract...的思考方式，得知要吸引他們，是需要 pureness of love，故答案為 **pureness**。

● **第 22 題**，The lecturer feels empathic and sympathetic for the **22.** who doesn't seem to know what love is，對應到 In *1984*, Winston is the protagonist and eventually falls in love with another girl，把數句聽力訊息進行整併可以得知答案就是 protagonist，故答案為 **protagonist**。

● **第 23 題**，He wants to direct his **23.** by solely focusing on his work, but he totally can't，對應到 He wants to shift the attention by solely focusing on his work, but he totally can't，direct 換成了 shift 但其他訊息不變，故答案為 **attention**。

● **第 24 題**，It is this kind of love that makes him **24.** to live，對應到 It is this kind of love that makes him desired to live，試題和聽力訊息完全一致，故答案為 **desired**。

- 第 **25** 題，Eventually they have a meeting on a Sunday afternoon, but he has no **25.**_____，對應到 eventually they have a date on a Sunday afternoon...that marks a great beginning for him...The next moment, the kiss and touch and other details all make it so believable. Winston's not having physical desire also alludes to the fact that he is totally in love with the girl，句意整併後耐心地聽到 physical desire 這個訊息，故答案為 **physical desire**。

- 第 **26** 題，Mr. Farebrother is the much better **26.**_____ because he is twenty times better than Fred，對應到 Fred was born in a wealthy family, but Mr. Farebrother is twenty times better than Fred, making him the much better prospect，句意整併加改寫，得出要填的是 prospect，而非 Fred，故答案為 **prospect**。

- 第 **27** 題，Mrs. Garth's metaphoric remark is due to Fred's increasingly **27.**_____ words，對應到 Mrs. Garth cannot say anything to her husband, and eventually can no longer endure Fred's increasingly vexing words，把 Mrs. Garth 講述的那段話換成了 metaphoric remark，不變的仍是 vexing words，故答案為 **vexing**。

- 第 **28** 題，Mr. Farebrother ironically happens to be Fred's **28.**_____，對應到 Bitter and hurtful remarks have led to Fred's sudden departure, and his jealousy towards Mr. Farebrother, who ironically happens to be his envoy，試題和聽力訊息完全一致，故答案為 **envoy**。

● **第 29 題**，Both **29.**_____ words and Mr. Farebrother's compliments about Mary's handwriting can be the clue for Fred's jealousy，對應到 His satirizing words towards Mrs. Farebrother and his sensitivity towards Mr. Farebrother's compliments about Mary's handwriting have demonstrated his jealousy，試題將原聽力訊息整合後改寫成 both 加後面兩個項目的描述，對應到 compliments 和 words 後，空格處很明顯是 satirizing，故答案為 **satirizing**。

● **第 30 題**，The thought of not having a fair chance has revealed Fred's **30.**_____ and pure love towards Mary，對應到 It's of no use, whatever I do, Mary, you are sure to marry Mr. Farebrother at last. Fred even thinks he doesn't have a fair chance...Fred's words all show his spontaneity and pure love towards Mary，試題有改寫，但是不變的仍是 Fred 對 Mary 的 spontaneity 和 pure love，故答案為 **spontaneity**。

⯈ 填空測驗

現在請再聽一次音檔，並做下列的測驗，檢視自己能否完成此填空測驗和強化自己聽力能力和拼字能力，降低並修正自己漏聽到聽力訊息的機會，大幅提升應考實力。

What is it about the first love that still fascinates most of us? No matter what the outcome about the first love, our **1.**＿＿＿＿＿ bring us back to pureness of the love. The innocence that makes it so special and memorable. Only the pureness of love can make people **2.**＿＿＿＿＿. For a great movie or a fascinating fiction, it is actually a vital element, otherwise, it is just two great looking people getting loved. That won't attract the attention of **3.**＿＿＿＿＿ and readers. Let alone making any money. For today's class, we are going to talk about its virginity by using two great **4.**＿＿＿＿＿, *1984* and *Middlemarch*.

In *1984*, Winston is the **5.**＿＿＿＿＿ and eventually falls in love with another girl. The point is he is married. I'm not recommending you to be the other woman. But I feel kind of **6.**＿＿＿＿＿ and **7.**＿＿＿＿＿ for him. The person who doesn't seem to know what love is and eventually gets married. ...they get married and have kids...until one day, they realize they don't love each other. Winston is already 39 years old, so I feel bad for him to be so late to realize what love is...

When he comes to the realization that he is in love with the girl, he wants to see her again. He wants to shift the **8.**＿＿＿＿＿ by solely focusing on his work, but he totally can't. It is this kind of love that makes him desired to live. He even has the thought of her young naked body. He has the crazy idea that the girl might change her mind or suddenly slip away from him...he feels tortured and sensitive...eventually they have a date on a Sunday **9.**_____...that marks a great beginning for him...

What makes me feel great about the development is Winston's candidness.

"I'm thirty-nine years old. I've got a wife that I can't get rid of. I've got varicose **10.**_____. I've got five false **11.**_____."

The next moment, the kiss and touch and other details all make it so believable. Winston's not having **12.**_____ desire also alludes to the fact that he is totally in love with the girl. It's the **13.**_____ of the pure love, a sharp contrast to things happening in an earlier chapter that Winston has sex with a woman who is 50 years old. He enters the room, and just does it...

In *Middlemarch*, we are going to talk about different aspect of the pure love. Some **14.**_____ such as jealousy are involved.

Love is not as simple as two people liking with each other. Other people, such as parents all play a key role, and in Fred's case, the greatest **15.**_____ comes from Lucy. Lucy obviously wants her girl, Mary, to get married with someone with a great deal of fortune. Fred was born in a **16.**_____ family, but Mr. Farebrother is twenty times better than Fred, making him the much better **17.**_____ _____. Mrs. Garth cannot say anything to her husband, and eventually can no longer endure Fred's increasingly vexing words. So she says "Yes, young people are usually **18.**_____ to everything but their own wishes, and seldom imagine how much those wishes cost others." Bitter and hurtful remarks have led to Fred's sudden **19.**_____, and his jealousy towards Mr. Farebrother, who ironically happens to be his envoy.

Now his **20.**_____ includes Mary's feelings towards him and Mr. Farebrother as a rival. His satirizing words towards Mrs. Farebrother and his **21.**_____ towards Mr. Farebrother's compliments about Mary's **22.**_____ have demonstrated his jealousy.

Mr. Farebrother is kind enough to let those two to have a space to talk to each other privately, but his **23.**_____ is mistaken by Fred. It's of no use, whatever I do, Mary, you are sure to marry Mr. Farebrother at last. Fred even thinks he doesn't have a fair **24.**_____ _____...

Fred's words all show his **25.**_____ and pure love towards Mary...it soon **26.**_____ that Fred is thinking it in the wrong way. absurdly **27.**_____. Fred is the one who proclaims his love towards Mary, and the fact that Mary is not in love with Mr. Farebrother making Fred feel **28.**_____.

And it is this pureness that makes Mary and Fred's part so refreshing and **29.**_____. After all, readers want a heart-felt story. Fred's **30.**_____ charm is obviously one of them.

參考答案

1. memories
2. resonated
3. moviegoers
4. bestsellers
5. protagonist
6. empathic
7. sympathetic
8. attention
9. afternoon
10. veins
11. teeth
12. physical
13. symbol
14. attributes
15. hindrance
16. wealthy
17. prospect
18. blind
19. departure
20. anxiety
21. sensitivity
22. handwriting
23. thoughtfulness
24. chance
25. spontaneity
26. transpires
27. adorable
28. relieved
29. delightful
30. dorky

Section 4

Questions 31-40

Write the correct letter, A-G, next to Questions 31-40

A Lucy

B Mr. Vincy

C Garth

D Mary

E Fred

F *How Will You Measure Your Life*

G *Where You Go Is Not Who You Will Be*

31. one's emotion cannot get back to normal
32. one's reaction related to sarcasm and bad connotations
33. one's career advice includes concentration on doing one thing
34. mention of three traits important for one's career
35. mention of choosing the career by weighing on something wrong
36. mention of one's lack of professional skills
37. mention of one's conviction contradictory to another
38. one's career can still be promising even if he lacks knowledge
39. mention of one's career that has to please both sides
40. mention of one's job will be ephemeral

影子跟讀練習 MP3 008

做完題目後，除了對答案知道錯的部分在哪外，更重要的是要修正自己聽力根本的問題，即聽力理解力和聽力專注力，聽力專注力的修正能逐步強化本身的聽力實力，所以現在請根據聽力內容「逐個段落」、「數個段落」或「整篇」進行跟讀練習，提升在實際考場時專注聽完每個訊息、定位出關鍵考點和搭配筆記回答完所有題目。Go!

For today's class, we are going to talk about *Middlemarch*, and fast-forward to chapter 56, since we don't have much time left...

"How happy is he born and taught. That serveth not another's will."

在今天的課堂，我們要談論的是《米德爾鎮的春天》，因為我們所剩的時間不多所以會飛快跳至第 56 章...

「不為他人意志而活的人，是多麼地幸福啊！」

What can be learnt from the old saying? Choosing a profession has never been easy, but I prefer to interpret this as "to be unaffected by others while choosing a profession has never been easy." Your parents, lovers, friends...and so on...all shape your viewpoints when it comes to choosing the path...

我們可以從這句古老的名言中學到什麼？選擇一個職業一直都不容易，但我更傾向將其詮釋成「在選擇一個職業時，不受其他人影響，一直都不容易。」當提到選擇職業道路時，你的父母、愛人、朋友...等等的，都會形塑著你的觀點...。

For most twentysomethings, they are uncertain about what they are going to do right after they graduate...That's why we are focusing on Fred's dilemma...Fred obviously doesn't know what he wants to do...that can be a downside for him, while people around his age are moving forward, and he remains stagnant...

對大多數的 20 多歲的人而言，他們不確定畢業後到底該從事什麼樣的工作...這也就是為什麼我們會將重點放在弗烈德的困境上...弗烈德顯然不知道自己想要從事什麼樣的工作...那對他來說會是不利的，當和自己有著近似年紀的人都往前邁進，而他仍裹足不前...。

Mary, whom Fred loves has a different opinion of what Fred should do in the future, so her viewpoint is in conflict with that of Fred's father. Mary will relinquish him if he chooses the work at the church.

瑪莉也就是弗烈德所愛的人，對於弗烈德未來該從事什麼樣的工作卻有著不同的看法，所以她的觀點和弗烈德父親的觀點是衝突的。瑪莉會因為弗烈德選擇教會的工作而放棄他。

The point is Fred has to find the future path. Certainly, there aren't any high-paying jobs that don't require special knowledge...that he clearly lacks? What can he do for a living if it's not the job at the church. Why doesn't he put his inner voice ahead of both Mary's and his father's.

重點是，弗烈德必須要找到未來的道路。可以確定的是，沒有一個高薪的工作是不需要專業知識的…這也是弗烈德顯然欠缺的…如果他不從事在教會的工作，那麼他要以什麼工作謀生呢？為什麼他不將自己的內在聲音，優於瑪莉和他父親的意見之上。

❶ profession 職業 [C]
❷ unaffected 不受影響的
❸ graduate 畢業
❹ dilemma 困境，進退兩難
❺ downside 不利；下降趨勢
❻ stagnant 不流動的，停滯的
❼ conflict 衝突，抵觸
❽ relinquish 放棄；撤出
❾ knowledge 知識
❿ inner voice 內在聲音

There is a chance accident at the field that guides Fred to think, this could be his employment for the future. The work at the field certainly doesn't need a bachelor's degree, but Fred shows his willingness to learn. From Garth's viewpoint, Fred is still young and has the time to lay the foundation.

在田野間，有個偶然的意外引導弗烈德去思考，這可能可以是他未來的工作。在田野間的工作確實不需要大學學歷，但是弗烈德顯示了自己的學習意願。從葛爾斯的觀點來說，弗烈德仍舊還年輕，是有時間能夠打好基礎。

（註：關於這點，弗烈德的求職態度真的好的沒話說，也不會因為自己

有大學學歷就看輕其他工作。當然，其他人也很願意幫他一把。）

To succinctly put what Garth has to say...and it's also important for those who are trying to find the first job...focus on doing one thing only and love your work...that's not only a great reminder for Fred, but for all twentysomethings...you cannot make a job hop whenever you want, thinking another job is more honorable or can be the right fit...and when you are entering your 30, you still don't know what you are going to be...while your classmates have accumulated 5-6 years of work experience in the same profession ready to shine...and you are either jobless or in another profession, learning from the very beginning, since you are a rookie in the field.

簡而概要地述說葛爾斯所想表達的...而這對於那些試圖要找到第一份工作的人來說也很重要...專注在只將一件事情做好，並且喜愛你的工作...這不僅僅是對弗烈德的最佳提醒，也是對那些 20 幾歲的人的建言...你不可能在每當你想這麼做的時候，就跳槽，認為下一份工作更令人尊敬或可能是最合適的...當你來到了 30 歲時，你仍然不知道自己想要成為什麼樣的人...而你的同班同學在同個領域中卻已經累積了 5-6 年的工作經驗，要準備發光發熱了...而你不是處於失業中或是在其他領域工作，從頭開始，因為你在該領域仍舊是個菜鳥。

This actually helps Fred get to know himself better. Now Fred knows he cannot do that if the job is a clergyman, eliminating the clergyman as the option of his profession... and at the same time, he can please Mary for not choosing the job at the Church. He just needs to figure out how to persuade his father for giving up the career as a clergyman.

實際上，這幫助了弗烈德更了解自己。現在，弗烈德知道他不能從事牧師的工作，將牧師從他職業選項中移除掉了...與此同時，他也能因為不選教會的工作而讓瑪莉感到滿意。他只需要了解要如何說服他父親，他選擇了放棄牧師當作自己的職涯。

❶ employment 僱用；受僱
❷ bachelor's degree 大學學歷
❸ willingness 自願；樂意
❹ foundation 基礎
❺ succinctly 簡潔地；簡便地
❻ reminder 提醒者，提醒物
❼ honorable 可尊敬的；高尚的
❽ accumulate 累積，積聚
❾ rookie 菜鳥
❿ clergyman 牧師

What's Mr. Vincy's reactions after hearing Fred's determination of working for Garth. "You've thrown away your education, and gone down a step in life, when I had given you the means of rising, that's all." "I wash my hands for you, only hope, when you have a son of your own he will make a better return for the pains you spend on him."

而溫奇在聽到弗烈德決定要替葛爾斯工作後的反應又是什麼？「你浪費了受過的教育，我給你機會向上爬，你卻選擇向下沉淪，就這樣。我再也不管你的事，只希望將來你有了兒子，他能用更好的方式來回報你的苦心。」

As for Fred's mother, Lucy, it is hard for her to regain her usual happiness. She clearly doesn't want Fred to marry Mary...

至於弗烈德的媽媽露西，她更難回復她往常的快樂了。她顯然不想要弗烈德和瑪莉結婚...。

In Fred's case, his father wants him to be a clergyman, a high-paying job. That's contrary to the advise given in *How Will You Measure Your Life* and *Where You Go Is Not Who You Will Be*.

在弗烈德的例子中，他爸爸想要他成為牧師，擁有一份高薪工作。那與《你如何衡量你的人生》以及《你讀哪所學校不會決定你未來會成為什麼樣的人》中所給予的建議是大相逕庭的。

In *How Will You Measure Your Life*, the author gives the advice of not using the hygiene factors as the primary criteria. Hygiene factors refer to high payment, compensation, and other benefits. Most of the peers of the Harvard professor had chosen careers by using hygiene factors, ending up unhappy. In *Where You Go Is Not Who You Will Be*, it mentions that "the career is built on carefully honed skills, ferocious work ethics, and good attitudes." Another concept relating to today's topic is if you do not know what you love chances are you won't be making a lot of money. And in Fred's case, choosing the career as a clergyman won't do him any good. He might be miserable at the job, and eventually quit the job after working for a while...astonishingly, both bestsellers seem to share identical wisdom with Eliot's work...I guess that's all for today.

在《你如何衡量你的人生》中，作者所給予的忠告是，別用保健因素當作主要的標準。保健因素指的是高薪、津貼和其他好處。這位哈佛教授的大多數同儕都使用了保健因素作為衡量工作的標準，最終卻不快樂。在《你讀哪所學校不會決定你未來會成為什麼樣的人》，它提到了「職涯是建立在幾經磨練的技術、驚人的工作道德和良好的態度上」。另一個與今天主題有關的是，如果你不知道你所愛的為何，很可能你無法賺取許多錢。在弗列德的例子中，選擇牧師當作職涯對他來說不會有任何好處。他可能在工作中苦不堪言，而最終在工作一陣子後就辭掉了工作…令人吃驚的是，兩本暢銷書似乎和艾略特的智慧是如出一轍的…我想今天的課就到此為止了。

❶ reaction 反應
❷ determination 決定
❸ education 教育
❹ regain 回復
❺ happiness 快樂
❻ hygiene 衛生；保健
❼ compensation 補償；賠償
❽ ferocious 兇猛的；殘忍的
❾ miserable 痛苦的；不幸的
❿ astonishingly 令人驚訝地

試題解析

- 第 **31** 題，one's emotion cannot get back to normal，對應到 As for Fred's mother, Lucy, it is hard for her to regain her usual happiness，指的就是她無法獲得原有的快樂了，emotion 指的就是 happiness，故答案要選 **A** Lucy。

- 第 **32** 題，one's reaction related to sarcasm and bad connotations，對應到 "You've thrown away your education, and gone down a step in life, when I had given you the means of rising, that's all." "I wash my hands for you, only hope, when you have a son of your own he will make a better return for the pains you spend on him"，將溫奇先生講的這兩句很沉重的話，改成 sarcasm and bad connotations，故答案要選 **B** Mr. Vincy。

- 第 **33** 題，one's career advice includes concentration on doing one thing，對應到 To succinctly put what Garth has to say...and it's also important for those who are trying to find the first job...focus on doing one thing only and love your work...that's not only a great reminder for Fred, but for all twentysomethings...，focus 對應到 concentration，故答案要選 **C** Garth。

- 第 **34** 題，mention of three traits important for one's career，對應到 In *Where You Go Is Not Who You Will Be*, it mentions that "the career is built on carefully honed skills, ferocious work ethics, and good attitudes"，three traits 對應到表列舉的三個項目，故答案要選 **G** *Where You Go Is Not Who You Will Be*。

- **第 35 題**，mention of choosing the career by weighing on something wrong，對應到 Most of the peers of the Harvard professor had chosen careers by using hygiene factors, ending up unhappy，weighing on something wrong 指的就是 using hygiene factors，故答案要選 **F** *How Will You Measure Your Life*。

- **第 36 題**，mention of one's lack of professional skills，對應到 The point is Fred has to find the future path. Certainly, there aren't any high-paying jobs that don't require special knowledge...that he clearly lacks，don't require special knowledge = one's lack of professional skills，故答案要選 **E** Fred。

- **第 37 題**，mention of one's conviction contradictory to another，對應到 Mary, whom Fred loves has a different opinion of what Fred should do in the future, so her viewpoint is in conflict with that of Fred's father，故答案要選 **D** Mary。

- **第 38 題**，one's career can still be promising even if he lacks knowledge，對應到 The work at the field certainly doesn't need a bachelor's degree, but Fred shows his willingness to learn. From Garth's viewpoint, Fred is still young and has the time to lay the foundation，故答案要選 **C** Garth。

● **第 39 題**，mention of one's career that has to please both sides，對應到 Mary, whom Fred loves has a different opinion of what Fred should do in the future, so her viewpoint is in conflict with that of Fred's father，其實就是暗指 Fred 要同時討好他爸爸和 Mary，也就是 both sides，故答案要選 **E** Fred。

● **第 40 題**，mention of one's job will be ephemeral，對應到 And in Fred's case, choosing the career as a clergyman won't do him any good. He might be miserable at the job, and eventually quit the job after working for a while...，ephemeral 指的就是工作期間會很短，等同於工作一陣子後又辭了，因為那仍然不是 Fred 想要的工作（在聽力訊息結尾），故答案要選 **E** Fred。

Instruction | MP3 008

現在請再聽一次音檔，並做下列的測驗，檢視自己能否完成此填空測驗和強化自己聽力能力和拼字能力，降低並修正自己漏聽到聽力訊息的機會，大幅提升應考實力。

What can be learnt from the old **1.**_____? Choosing a profession has never been easy, but I prefer to interpret this as "to be **2.**_____ by others while choosing a profession has never been easy." Your parents, lovers, friends...and so on...all shape your viewpoints when it comes to choosing the path...

For most twentysomethings, they are uncertain about what they are going to do right after they graduate...That's why we are focusing on Fred's **3.**_____

...Fred obviously doesn't know what he wants to do...that can be a downside for him, while people around his age are moving forward, and he remains **4.**_____...Mary, whom Fred loves has a different opinion of what Fred should do in the future, so her viewpoint is in conflict with that of Fred's father. Mary will **5.**_____ him if he chooses the work at the church.

The point is Fred has to find the future path. Certainly, there aren't any high-paying jobs that don't require special **6.**_____...that he clearly lacks? What can he do for a living if it's not the job at the **7.**_____. Why doesn't he put his inner voice ahead of both Mary's and his father's.

There is a chance accident at the field that guides Fred to think, this could be his **8.**_____ for the future. The work at the field certainly doesn't need a **9.**_____ degree, but Fred shows his willingness to learn. From Garth's viewpoint, Fred is still young and has the time to lay the **10.**_____.

To **11.**_____ put what Garth has to say...and it's also important for those who are trying to find the first job...focus on doing one thing only and love your work...that's not only a great **12.**_____ for Fred, but for all twentysomethings...you cannot make a job hop whenever you want, thinking another job is more **13.**_____ or can be the right fit...and when you are entering your 30, you still don't know what you are going to be...while your **14.**_____ have accumulated 5-6 years of work experience in the same profession ready to shine...and you are either **15.**_____ or in another profession, learning from the very beginning, since you are a **16.**_____ in the field.

This actually helps Fred get to know himself better. Now Fred knows he cannot do that if the job is a clergyman, eliminating the clergyman as the option of his **17.**_____... and at the same time, he can please Mary for not choosing the job at the Church. He just needs to figure out how to **18.**_____ his father for giving up the career as a clergyman.

What's Mr. Vincy's reactions after hearing Fred's **19.**_____ of working for Garth. "You've thrown away your **20.**_____, and gone down a step in life, when I had given you the means of rising, that's all." "I wash my hands for you, only hope, when you have a son of your own he will make a better return for the pains you spend on him."

As for Fred's mother, Lucy, it is hard for her to regain her usual **21.**_____.

In Fred's case, his father wants him to be a clergyman, a high-paying job. That's contrary to the advise given in *How Will You Measure Your Life* and *Where You Go Is Not Who You Will Be*.

In *How Will You Measure Your Life*, the author gives the advice of not using the hygiene factors as the primary **22.**_____. Hygiene factors refer to high **23.**_____, compensation, and other benefits. Most of the peers of the **24.**_____ professor had chosen careers by using hygiene factors, ending up unhappy. In *Where You Go Is Not Who You Will Be*, it mentions that "the career is built on carefully honed skills, **25.**_____ work ethics, and good **26.**_____." Another **27.**_____ relating to today's topic is if you do not know what you love chances are you won't be making a lot of money. And in Fred's case, choosing the career as a **28.**_____ won't do him any good. He might be **29.**_____ at the job, and eventually quit the job after working for a while...astonishingly, both bestsellers seem to share identical **30.**_____ with Eliot's work...I guess that's all for today.

參考答案

1. saying		**2.** unaffected	
3. dilemma		**4.** stagnant	
5. relinquish		**6.** knowledge	
7. church		**8.** employment	
9. bachelor's		**10.** foundation	
11. succinctly		**12.** reminder	
13. honorable		**14.** classmates	
15. jobless		**16.** rookie	
17. profession		**18.** persuade	
19. determination		**20.** education	
21. happiness		**22.** criteria	
23. payment		**24.** Harvard	
25. ferocious		**26.** attitudes	
27. concept		**28.** clergyman	
29. miserable		**30.** wisdom	

Section 1 Questions 1-10
Complete the Notes below
Write No More than 2 Words for each answer

About the vase:
- Waiter: don't open it.
- In actuality: numerous vases behind the curtain.
- Wild conjecture: might be **1.**_____ .
- To make the scene scarier:
- one of them uses **2.**_____ from last year's Halloween party
- one of them has decided to **3.**_____ .

Conversation with the waiter:
- we just had a glass of champagne and the **4.**_____ came really close...
- utilize the **5.**_____ if they need the waiter.

Smoke:
- The color of the smoke: **6.**_____.
- Causes **7.**_____.
- Drink from the **8.**_____ might help...although it might generate extra cost

Remove spiders:

They have **9.**_____ in the bag, but using it actually makes things worse.

Suggestions:
- go to the lobby, but the door is locked
- hide in the **10.**_____.
- grab our bags and run
- press the button

- 第 **1** 題，Wild conjecture: might be **1.**_____，對應到 they are...and let me guess... worms in those vases...**caterpillars**，Wild conjecture 對應到 let me guess，故答案為 **caterpillars**。

- 第 **2** 題，one of them uses **2.**_____ from last year's Halloween party，對應到 what about this...scary **music** from last year's Halloween party...，試題和聽力訊息完全一致，故答案為 **music**。

- 第 **3** 題，one of them has decided to **3.**_____，對應到 then I guess I have no choice but **scream** while opening it...，有進行改寫，「不得不」對應到「已決定要...」故答案為 **scream**。

- 第 **4** 題，just had a glass of champagne and the **4.**_____ came really close...，對應到 we just had a glass of champagne and the **killer bee** came really close...，試題和聽力訊息完全一致，故答案為 **killer bee**。

- 第 **5** 題，utilize the **5.**_____ if they need the waiter 對應到 if you do need me? Just use the **old telephone**...and press the button "die"...，utilize 對應到 use，故答案為 **old telephone**。

- 第 **6** 題，The color of the smoke: **6.**_____，對應到 Flickering **purple** smoke rising from it，所以 smoke 的顏色為紫色，故答案為 **purple**。

- 第 **7** 題，Causes **7.**_____，對應到 I'm feeling **dizzy**...，這題有進行改寫且需要將聽到的字更改成符合試題文法的答案，要改成名詞，故答案為 **dizziness**。

- 第 **8** 題，Drink from the **8.**_____ might help...although it might generate extra cost，對應到 can you go get some drink from the **refrigerator**，試題有更改文字表達，但是答案不變，由 drink 可以協助對應到訊息，故答案為 **refrigerator**。

- 第 **9** 題，They have **9.**_____ in the bag, but using it actually makes things worse，對應到 Just get rid of them...I have **insecticide** in the bag，這題有進行改寫，濃縮數句聽力訊息，接在後句，但前面的試題完全沒更動，跟聽力訊息完全一樣，故答案為 **insecticide**。

- 第 **10** 題，hide in the **10.**_____，對應到 I think it is...we have no choice to hide in the **closet**（試題並未改寫），故答案為 **closet**。

147

影子跟讀練習 MP3 009

做完題目後，除了對答案知道錯的部分在哪外，更重要的是要修正自己聽力根本的問題，即聽力理解力和聽力專注力，聽力專注力的修正能逐步強化本身的聽力實力，所以現在請根據聽力內容「逐個段落」、「數個段落」或「整篇」進行跟讀練習，提升在實際考場時專注聽完每個訊息、定位出關鍵考點和搭配筆記回答完所有題目。Go!

| B |

Don't open the vase...I mean I just don't like his tone...

| B |

別打開花瓶...我指的是，我還真不喜歡他的語調...

| C |

and which vase, obviously there are plenty of vases behind the curtain...

| C |

還有到底是哪個花瓶呢？窗簾後面有許多花瓶呢？

| B |

Oh the vase on the table is sealed. Are they all fastened?

| B |

噢！在桌上的花瓶是密封的。所有的花瓶都被封口了嗎？

| C |

I think they are...and let me guess... worms in those vases...**caterpillars**?

| C |

我想是吧...讓我猜看看...那些花瓶裡頭有蟲...毛毛蟲？

| B |

why don't we just open the one on the table?

| B |

為什麼我們不打開桌上這個花瓶呢？

| C |

then you do it...since you are the one who makes that kind of suggestions...

| C |

那...你來打開...既然是你提的主意

| B |

fine...I might be slightly afraid of scorpions...opening a vase is not that scary...

| B |

好吧...我可能對於毒蠍有些微的恐懼...打開花瓶沒有那麼恐怖好嗎？...

| C |

what about this...scary **music** from last year's Halloween party...

| C |

那這樣呢...播放去年萬聖節的駭人音樂...

| B |

then I guess I have no choice but **scream** while opening it...

| B |

那...我想我沒得選擇了，只能邊打開時邊叫...

| A |

(knocking on the door) Is everything ok?

| A |

（敲擊房門的聲音）裡頭還好嗎？

| C |

Everything is fine...we just had a glass of champagne and the **killer bee** came really close...

| C |

一切都好...我們喝了杯香檳，有隻殺人蜂卻靠得非常近...

| A |

Ok...if you need me? Just use the **old telephone**...and press the button "die"...

| A |

好的，如果你們需要我的話？就使用舊電話...然後按下「死亡」鍵

| B |

die?...what do you mean?

| B |

「死亡」？...你指的是什麼啊？

| C |

I think he is gone already...what should we do?

| C |

我想他已經走掉了...我們該怎麼辦？

| B |

What's that smell? From the vase?

| B |

那是什麼味道啊？從花瓶傳來的？

| C |

Flickering **purple** smoke rising from it

| C |

有道搖曳的紫煙往上飄起。

| B |

Is it toxic? Do we have to retreat to the underpass?

| B |

煙有毒嗎？我們是否必須要撤退到通道裡頭了？

| C |

Absolutely not...staying here is actually safer?

| C |

當然不能...待在這裡實際上更為安全吧？

| B |

I'm feeling **dizzy**...can you go get some drink from the **refrigerator**?

| B |

我感到有些暈眩...你可以從冰箱裡取些飲料嗎？

| C |

But that's going to cost us extra money......let's see what's in there...two bottles of red wine...three blue lobsters and two large spiders...and where are these spiders crawling towards?

| C |

但是這要多花我們額外的錢唉！...讓我看看...冰箱裡有些什麼...兩瓶紅酒...三隻藍色龍蝦,還有兩隻大蜘蛛...這些蜘蛛要爬去哪啊！

| B |

Just get rid of them...I have **insecticide** in the bag.

| B |

就...除掉他們...我的袋子裡有殺蟲劑。

| C |

I don't think it's working...I think they have become larger...than they used to...

| C |

我不認為殺蟲劑有發揮作用...我看蜘蛛已經變得更大隻了...比起他們原先更大隻了...

| B |

Let's go to the lobby and get some help...don't tell me that the door is locked...

| B |

讓我們去大廳尋求一些幫助...別跟我說門被鎖上了...

| C |

I think it is...we have no choice but to hide in the **closet**?

| C |

我想門被鎖上了...我們不得不藏在衣櫃裡頭嗎？

| B |

that's not the greatest hiding place...we are not the other woman...think something better...

| B |

衣櫃不是最佳的藏身所...何況我們又不是小三...想些更好的辦法吧...

| C |

grab our bags and run...with your dizziness, obviously we can't fight those spiders...

| C |

拿起我們的袋子，然後逃跑...以你現在暈眩的狀態，顯然我們打不贏那些蜘蛛...

| B |

there is actually something that you can do...press the button...

| B |

確實有些是你能做的事...按下那按鍵...。

| C |

Ok...I think I will just press live?

| C |

好的...我想我會按「存活」？

| A |

Are you guys still in there? Are you guys feeling Ok...Do you have the crucifix? Using it to tackle the spider...

| A |

你們還在裡頭嗎？你們都覺得還好嗎？你們有十字架嗎？用十字架去對付蜘蛛...。

| **Instruction** | MP3 **001**

現在請再聽一次音檔,並做下列的測驗,檢視自己能否完成此填空測驗和強化自己聽力能力和拼字能力,降低並修正自己漏聽到聽力訊息的機會,大幅提升應考實力。

| **B** |

Don't **1.**_____ the vase...I mean I just don't like his **2.**_____...

| **C** |

and which vase, obviously there are **3.**_____ of vases behind the **4.**_____...

| **B** |

Oh the vase on the table is **5.**_____. Are they all **6.**_____?

| **C** |

I think they are...and let me guess... **7.**_____ in those vases...**8.**_____?

| **B** |

why don't we just open the one on the **9.**_____?

| C |

then you do it...since you are the one who makes that kind of **10.**_____...

| B |

fine...I might be slightly afraid of **11.**_____...opening a vase is not that scary...

| C |

what about this...scary music from last year's **12.**_____ party...

| B |

then I guess I have no choice but **13.**_____ while opening it...

| A |

(knocking on the door) Is everything ok?

| C |

Everything is fine...we just had a glass of **14.**_____ and the killer **15.**_____ came really close...

| A |

Ok...if you need me? Just use the old **16.**_____...and press the button "die"...

| B |

die?...what do you mean?

| C |

I think he is gone already...what should we do?

| B |

What's that smell? From the vase?

| C |

Flickering **17.**_____ **18.**_____ rising from it

| B |

Is it toxic? Do we have to retreat to the underpass?

| C |

Absolutely not...staying here is actually **19.**_____?

| B |

I'm feeling dizzy...can you go get some drink from the **20.**_____ _____?

| C |

But that's going to cost us extra **21.**_____......let's see what's in there...two bottles of red **22.**_____...three blue **23.**_____ and two large spiders...and where are these spiders **24.**_____ _____ towards?

| B |

Just get rid of them...I have **25.** _____ in the bag.

| C |

I don't think it's working...I think they have become larger...than they used to...

| B |

Let's go to the lobby and get some help...don't tell me that the door is locked...

| C |

I think it is...we have no choice to hide in the **26.** _____ ?

| B |

that's not the greatest **27.** _____ place...we are not the other woman...think something better...

| C |

grab out bags and run...with your **28.** _____, obviously we can't fight those spiders...

| B |

there is actually something that you can do...press the **29.** _____ ...

| C |

Ok...I think I will just press live?

| A |

　　...Are you guys still in there? Are you guys feeling Ok...Do you have the crucifix? Using it to tackle the **30.**＿＿＿＿＿＿?...

| 參考答案 |

1. open
2. tone
3. plenty
4. curtain
5. sealed
6. fastened
7. worms
8. caterpillars
9. table
10. suggestions
11. scorpions
12. Halloween
13. scream
14. champagne
15. bee
16. telephone
17. purple
18. smoke
19. safer
20. refrigerator
21. money
22. wine
23. lobsters
24. crawling
25. insecticide
26. closet
27. hiding
28. dizziness
29. button
30. spider

Section 2
Questions 11-20

Write the correct letter, A-G, next to Questions 11-20

A *Pride and Prejudice*

B *Gone with the Wind*

C *1984*

D *The History of Tom Jones, a Founding*

E *Gone with the Wind* and *1984*

F lecturer

G other people's perception

11. Youth is not permanent
12. Countenances created by genes will be affected by other factors
13. genes determine most of people's fate from birth
14. With the conviction that good-looking people are not the winner.
15. To gainsay the fact that beauty is luscious is ridiculous.
16. One's destitution will be the downside for one's inherent look.
17. the attainment of an optimum stage in a short time
18. Penchant for choosing the spouse much more attractive than they are
19. Practicality comes first, when it comes to sustaining a marriage
20. All men are created equal, when it comes to making a living

影子跟讀練習 MP3 010

做完題目後，除了對答案知道錯的部分在哪外，更重要的是要修正自己聽力根本的問題，即聽力理解力和聽力專注力，聽力專注力的修正能逐步強化本身的聽力實力，所以現在請根據聽力內容「逐個段落」、「數個段落」或「整篇」進行跟讀練習，提升在實際考場時專注聽完每個訊息、定位出關鍵考點和搭配筆記回答完所有題目。Go!

Today's topic is appearance and youth. Being youthful means much better looking, not getting aged...I think most of you would agree with me on this. Even though there is a saying that "don't judge a book by its cover" or you have to value the inner beauty...we still cannot downgrade the physical attractiveness. In *The History of Tom Jones, a Founding*, there is even a saying that supports the attribute of beauty. "to deny that beauty is an agreeable object to the eye, and even worthy some admiration, would be false and foolish." After all, people want to be around with good-looking people or they fancy to have the spouse, much better looking than they are.

今天的主題是外表和青春。富有青春活力意謂著更加好看，沒有老化徵狀...我想你們大多數的人會同意我所說的這點。即使有個諺語說道「人不可貌相」或是你必須要重視內在美...我們仍無法小看外在吸引力。在《湯姆·瓊斯》書中，甚至有個俗諺是支持美貌這個特質的：「美麗的容貌確實賞心悅目，也值得稱頌，否認這點，未免流於虛偽可笑。」畢竟，人們想要周遭圍繞著好看的人或是他們喜愛比起他們條件來說，相貌更為出眾的配偶。

In *Gone with the Wind*, Scarlett is certainly aware of how transient one's beauty can be, so she wants to seize the time while she is still good-looking. In one of the illustrious British novels, *1984*, it also mentions beauty is transitory through the observation of the protagonist, Winston.

在《亂世佳人》中,思嘉麗確實察覺到一個人的美貌有多短暫,所以她想在還好看的時候把握時機。在著名的英國小說《1984》中,也透過小說主角溫斯頓的觀察提及了美貌的短暫。

❶ appearance 外表
❷ agree 同意
❸ downgrade 降低,貶低
❹ attractiveness 吸引力;迷惑力
❺ attribute 特性,特質
❻ agreeable 令人愉快的,宜人的
❼ admiration 欽佩,讚美
❽ fancy 愛好;迷戀
❾ transient 短暫的
❿ transitory 短暫的

"She had had her momentary flowering, a year perhaps, of wild-rose beauty and then she had suddenly swollen like a fertilized fruit and grown hard and red and coarse..."

「她這朵鮮花曾經短暫盛開過,或許只有一年,綻放出野玫瑰的美,然後突然之間,她就像顆授了精的果實,變得堅硬,紅潤又粗糙...。」

Winston laments that from youthful to old, it's like within seconds. Even with the plastics surgery nowadays, we still cannot make our beauty permanently lasts. Still people are envious of those with attractive looks, thinking that genes determine most of people's fate from birth. Good-looking people enjoy the spotlight from childhood to adulthood, garnering attention from everyone. They can have many dates and multiple options.

溫斯頓悲嘆從年輕到老年，就像在彈指之間。即使現今有外科手術，我們仍無法讓美貌永久保持住。人們仍羨慕那些外貌引人注目的人，認為從打出生開始基因就決定了大多數人的命運。好看的人從童年到成年享有眾人的目光，獲取每個人的注意。他們可以有許多約會對象和眾多選擇。

From this viewpoint, they are the winner, but I think not really...why? Another viewpoint putting forward that actually makes people with mundane looks more confident. There is a saying that good-looking people's victory is fleeting, especially after 35. Before the age of 35, it's what your parents give you. So after 35, you can hardly find someone who is still good-looking.

從這個觀點來看，他們是贏家，但是我認為不是這麼回事...為什麼呢？另一個所提出的觀點實際上讓相貌平凡的人看了之後會更有自信。有個俗諺是這麼說的，好看的人的勝利是短暫的，尤其在過了 35 歲之後。在 35 歲之前，外貌是你父母賦予你的。所以在 35 歲後，你更難找到外貌仍舊好看的人。

For those who are still physically attractive, it is because they are kind-hearted or they do possess inner beauty. Inner beauty does play a key role. Not to mention, our countenance does change from time to time. People who have committed a heinous crime exhibits an evil look on their face. Gradually, it ruins the previous good-looking face. From this standpoint, it actually makes us feel better, and instead work on the inner beauty. Work stress and other factors can also affect how we look, so we don't have to be envious of others.

對於那些外貌仍具吸引力者，這是因為他們有顆善良的心或者是他們確實有內在美。內在美確實扮演了一個關鍵的角色。更別說，我們的容貌確實會隨著時間而改變。犯下可恨的罪刑的人在他們的臉上彰顯出了邪惡之相。逐漸地，毀損了先前好看的樣貌了。從這個觀點來看，這確實讓我們覺得心情更舒暢了，而取而代之的是將焦點著重在內在美上。工作壓力和其他因素也都會影響我們看起來如何，所以我們不需要去羨慕別人。

❶ lament 哀悼，悲痛
❷ surgery 外科
❸ permanently 永久地；長期不變地
❹ envious 嫉妒的；羨慕的
❺ garner 收藏；獲得
❻ multiple 多樣的
❼ mundane 平凡的; 乏味的
❽ victory 勝利；戰勝
❾ countenance 面容，臉色
❿ heinous 可憎的；兇惡的

In *Pride and Prejudice*, there is also a saying: "they are young in the ways of the world, and not yet open to the mortifying conviction that handsome young men must have something to live on as well as the plain."

在《傲慢與偏見》，也有句俗諺說道：「他們年紀尚小，涉世未深，還不知道一個惱人的道理：美男子就跟普通人一樣，也是要謀生過日子的。」

Whether you are handsome or not, you have to work. Poor people with handsome looks can still waste the gene, since doing strenuous work can easily wear out the good-looking face. It's actually related to another topic...it's about choosing a mate. One might wonder should I choose the one who is good-looking or the one with the normal look? The point is you have to face the fact that you have to make a living. So even after getting married, you have to be able to live the lives with your spouse. I guess you have to be practical, choosing someone who is industrious and willing to support you, rather than focusing the attention on the look...I guess that's all for today's class.

不論你英俊與否，你都必須要工作。窮人有著英俊的外表仍可能浪費了基因，因為做費力粗重的活很容易就耗盡一張好看的面容。這實際上也與另一個主題有關...就是關於選擇伴侶。一個人可能會去想，我該選擇一個好看的對象或者是一個相貌平凡的人呢？重點是，你必須要面對的現實是，你需要謀生。所以即使結婚了，你必須要能夠與你的配偶能夠相處生活。我想你就必須要更為實際點，選擇一個更勤奮工作並且願意支持你的人，而非將焦點放在外貌上...我想今天的課堂就到此為止了。

❶ mortifying 令人感到屈辱的

❷ conviction 確信，信念

❸ strenuous 費勁的，費力的

❹ spouse 配偶

❺ practical 實際的；實用的

❻ industrious 勤勉的，勤奮的

● **第 11 題**，Youth is not permanent，對應到 In *Gone with the Wind*, Scarlett is certainly aware of how transient one's beauty can be, so she wants to seize the time while she is still good-looking. In one of the illustrious British novels, *1984*, it also mentions beauty is transitory through the observation of the protagonist, Winston，transient 和 transitory 都是關鍵訊息，故答案要選 **E** *Gone with the Wind* and *1984*。

● **第 12 題**，Countenances created by genes will be affected by other factors，對應到 Work stress and other factors can also affect how we look, so we don't have to be envious of others，這句是講者的陳述，故答案要選 **F** lecturer。

● **第 13 題**，genes determine most of people's fate from birth，對應到 Still people are envious of those with attractive looks, thinking that genes determine most of people's fate from birth. Good-looking people enjoy the spotlight from childhood to adulthood, garnering attention from everyone，關鍵字是 thinking that，代表是那些人認為的，故答案要選 **G** other people's perception。

● **第 14 題**，With the conviction that good-looking people are not the winner，對應到 From this viewpoint, they are the winner, but I think not really...why，這句是講者的陳述，故答案要選 **F** lecturer。

● 第 **15** 題，To gainsay the fact that beauty is luscious is ridiculous.，對應到"to deny that beauty is an agreeable object to the eye, and even worthy some admiration, would be false and foolish."，故答案要選 **D** *The History of Tom Jones, a Founding*。

● 第 **16** 題，One's destitution will be the downside for one's inherent look，對應到 Poor people with handsome looks can still waste the gene, since doing strenuous work can easily wear out the good-looking face，這句是講者的陳述，故答案要選 **F** lecturer。

● 第 **17** 題，the attainment of an optimum stage in a short time，對應到 "She had had her momentary flowering, a year perhaps, of wild-rose beauty and then she had suddenly swollen like a fertilized fruit and grown hard and red and coarse..."，故答案要選 **C** *1984*。

● 第 **18** 題，Penchant for choosing the spouse much more attractive than they are，對應到 After all, people want to be around with good-looking people or they fancy to have the spouse, much better looking than they are，這句是講者的陳述，故答案要選 **F** lecturer。

● 第 **19** 題，Practicality comes first, when it comes to sustaining a marriage，對應到 I guess you have to be **practical**, choosing someone who is industrious and willing to support you, rather than focusing the attention on the look...，這句是講者的陳述，故答案要選 **F** lecturer。

● **第 20 題**，All men are created equal, when it comes to making a living，對應到 In *Pride and Prejudice*, there is also a saying: "they are young in the ways of the world, and not yet open to the mortifying conviction that handsome young men must have something to live on as well as the plain"，故答案要選 **A** *Pride and Prejudice*。

▶▶ 填空測驗

| Instruction | MP3 010

　　現在請再聽一次音檔，並做下列的測驗，檢視自己能否完成此填空測驗和強化自己聽力能力和拼字能力，降低並修正自己漏聽到聽力訊息的機會，大幅提升應考實力。

Today's topic is **1.**＿＿＿＿＿＿ and youth. Being **2.**＿＿＿＿＿＿ means much better looking, not getting aged...I think most of you would agree with me on this. Even though there is a saying that "don't judge a book by its cover" or you have to value the inner beauty...we still cannot downgrade the physical **3.**＿＿＿＿＿＿. In *The History of Tom Jones, a Founding*, there is even a saying that supports the attribute of beauty. "to deny that beauty is an **4.**＿＿＿＿＿＿ object to the eye, and even worthy some **5.**＿＿＿＿＿＿, would be false and foolish." After all, people want to be around with good-looking people or they **6.**＿＿＿＿＿＿ to have the spouse, much better looking than they are.

In *Gone with the Wind*, Scarlett is certainly aware of how **7.**＿＿＿＿ ＿＿＿ one's beauty can be, so she wants to seize the time while she is still good-looking. In one of the illustrious British novels, *1984*, it also mentions beauty is **8.**＿＿＿＿＿＿ through the observation of the protagonist, Winston.

"She had had her **9.**＿＿＿＿＿＿ flowering, a year perhaps, of wild-rose beauty and then she had suddenly swollen like a **10.**＿＿＿ ＿＿＿ fruit and grown hard and red and coarse..."

Even with the plastics **11.**_____ nowadays, we still cannot make our beauty permanently lasts. Still people are envious of those with **12.**_____ looks, thinking that genes determine most of people's **13.**_____ from birth. Good-looking people enjoy the spotlight from childhood to **14.**_____, garnering attention from everyone.

From this viewpoint, they are the **15.**_____, but I think not really...why? Another viewpoint putting forward that actually makes people with **16.**_____ looks more confident. There is a saying that good-looking people's victory is **17.**_____, especially after **35.** Before the age of 35, it's what your parents give you.

Inner beauty does play a key role. Not to mention, our **18.**_____ does change from time to time. People who have committed a **19.**_____ crime exhibits an evil look on they face. From this standpoint, it actually makes us feel better, and instead work on the **20.**_____ beauty. Work stress and other factors can also affect how we look, so we don't have to be **21.**_____ of others.

In *Pride and Prejudice*, there is also a saying: "they are young in the ways of the world, and not yet open to the mortifying **22.**_____ that handsome young men must have something to live on as well as the **23.**_____."

Poor people with **24.**_____ looks can still waste the **25.**_____, since doing **26.**_____ work can easily wear out the good-looking face. One might wonder should I choose the one who is good-looking or the one with the **27.**_____ look? The point is you have to face the fact that you have to make a living. So even after getting married, you have to be able to live the lives with your **28.**_____ _____. I guess you have to be **29.**_____, choosing someone who is **30.**_____ and willing to support you, rather than focusing the attention on the look...

| 參考答案 |

1. appearance
2. youthful
3. attractiveness
4. agreeable
5. admiration
6. fancy
7. transient
8. transitory
9. momentary
10. fertilized
11. surgery
12. attractive
13. fate
14. adulthood
15. winner
16. mundane
17. fleeting
18. countenance
19. heinous
20. inner
21. envious
22. conviction
23. plain
24. handsome
25. gene
26. strenuous
27. normal
28. spouse
29. practical
30. industrious

Section 4
Questions 21-30

Write the correct letter, A-K, next to Questions 21-30

A Serenoa

B Avlora

C Medina

D Corentin

E Decimal

F the Aelfric

G the warship of the Aesfrost

H Minister Lyla

I *The Aelfric Method in Practice*

J a Frederica route

K the true ending route

21. Despite previous acquaintance, one will act stringently
22. With formidable skills in battle, one's join still cannot make the journey smooth
23. One's abandonment eventually gets compensated
24. Realization of the constraint of staying in a particular country
25. One's confidence in himself or herself plays a role in how one gets ahead
26. Seeking the truth behind what is the component of "the Aelfric"

27. Plays a weighty role in exploding the warship of the Aesfrost
28. Involves the method of manufacturing a material
29. The greatest warrior will be added to your team
30. Whose magic involves immobilization that can greatly slash down the team's mobility

做完題目後，除了對答案知道錯的部分在哪外，更重要的是要修正自己聽力根本的問題，即聽力理解力和聽力專注力，聽力專注力的修正能逐步強化本身的聽力實力，所以現在請根據聽力內容「逐個段落」、「數個段落」或「整篇」進行跟讀練習，提升在實際考場時專注聽完每個訊息、定位出關鍵考點和搭配筆記回答完所有題目。Go!

There are several formidable skirmishes throughout the game, *Triangle Strategy*, even if you are not playing hard mode. Gamers choosing "normal" still find themselves having a hard time in key battles, especially in chapter 7, *Not a Word, My Friend*. Players are stuck with having in a war with one of the greatest warriors, Avlora, the awesome female fighter, whose attack can slash most characters' 70% to 80% HP, making most discouraging to have a flight with her head-on, and almost all characters cannot endure her attack twice...during the battle with Avlora, not using the fire trap to win the game presents a great challenge for most gamers even under "normal" by using only 10 units....however, we are not talking about Avlora today, since she has garnered too much of the limelight from most players...if so who shall we be talking to...

即使你不是玩困難模式，在三角戰略遊戲中，也有幾場戰鬥難以應付。選擇「普通難度」的玩家仍會發現他們在關鍵戰役中步履艱難，尤其是第七章〈吾友，不必多言〉。玩家會在與其中一位偉大的戰鬥者艾芙蘿拉交戰時進入膠著，艾芙蘿拉這位出色的女性戰鬥家的攻擊能夠削減我方角色血量70%至80%，讓大多數人對於與她正面交鋒心灰氣餒，而幾乎所有角色都無法承受她兩次的攻擊...在與艾芙蘿拉戰鬥時，不使用火陷陷阱要贏得這場戰役，對大多數即使以普通難度來進行遊戲的玩家，且僅能使用 10 個單位的玩家來說都造成了很大的挑戰...然而，我們今天卻不會談論艾芙蘿拉，因為她已經獲得了大多數玩家的注目了...如果是這樣的話，那我們該討論的人會是誰呢？

（註 1：不使用火焰陷阱是達成真結局的條件之一。）
（註 2：每個單位指的是能派上場的角色人數。大多數戰役都有設定條件和只能派所擁有的角色中其中 10 個角色上場。）

To be honest, most gamers will play this game for more than one round, and actually there are five endings throughout the game...however, only one of them will be the true ending. In two of these endings...near the very end, you are bound to encounter Minister Lyla, the sorceress, with the ability that you cannot take it too lightly...

老實說，大多數的玩家在玩這款遊戲時會玩不只一輪，而實際上在這款遊戲中，有五個結局...然而，這之中只有一個會是真結局。在這些結局中的其中兩個結局裡...幾乎接近遊戲尾聲時，你會遇到大魔法師萊拉閣下，他有著讓你無法輕視的能力...。

And if you meet all the criteria for the true ending, you will get Avlora in chapter 17, but if you think having the greatest warrior like Avlora, your road to beat one of the final battles with Minister Lyla will be smooth, then you are completely mistaken...

而如果你都符合了所有真結局所要求的條件的話，你在第 17 章將會獲得艾芙蘿拉加入，但是如果你認為有像艾芙蘿拉這樣出色的角色，你在與萊拉閣下的最終戰役中就能順利打敗他，那麼你就大錯特錯了...。

❶ formidable 難以應付的

❷ skirmish 戰鬥

❸ warrior 鬥士，戰士

❹ awesome 出色的

❺ discouraging 令人沮喪的

❻ limelight 眾人注目的中心

❼ sorceress 女魔法師

❽ lightly 輕輕地，輕微地

❾ criteria 標準

❿ completely 完整地；完全地

And who is Lyla anyway...she is the head of Ministry of Medicine at Holy State of Hyzante...whom our main character, Serenoa, meets at the very beginning of the story...

說了這麼多，那到底誰是萊拉呢？...她是聖海桑德大教國醫法院的院長...也就是我們的主角瑟雷諾亞在故事初遇到的人...。

Under two circumstances, you will have a fight with Lyla. The first one is choosing a Frederica route, and the second one is the true ending route...

在兩種情況下，你會與萊拉戰鬥。第一個是你選擇了芙德麗卡路線，而第二個則是你選擇了真結局路線...。

During these routes, players will still have to go through several scenes that will require them to evaluate their relationships with Aesfrost and the Holy State of Hyzante...there are no right or wrong answers...just considerations for the benefit of the country...

在這些路線期間，玩家會經歷幾個場景，要求他們要評估自己和艾斯弗斯特公國與聖海桑德大教國的關係...當中並沒有對或錯的答案...只是必須考慮當下對本國的益處...

In the middle part of the game, most will get an ally with the Holy State of Hyzante to slash down the power of Aesfrost...that will include another three choices...simply put, in one of the cooperative schemes with the Holy State of Hyzante, gamers have to defeat all Aesfrost forces and then use the formidable substance to detonate the warship of the Aesfrost...and why do we talk about the substance...because it is relevant to one of the battles with Lyla...the formidable substance is purple, and is called "the Aelfric"...at that time, we can only know it's powerful enough to destroy the warship of the Aesfrost...

在遊戲中段時，大多數人會與聖海桑德大教國結盟以削弱艾斯弗斯特公國的實力...這會包含另外的三個選擇...簡言之，在與聖海桑德大教國的其中一個合作計畫中，玩家必須要擊敗艾斯弗斯特公國的軍力，而接著使用令人畏懼的物質使艾斯弗斯特的戰船爆炸...，為什麼我們會談論這個物質呢？...因為這與我們和萊拉的其中一個戰役有關聯...這個可怕的物質是紫色的，而其被稱為「艾弗里克」...在那個時候，我們僅能知道其威力大到能夠毀掉艾斯弗斯特公國的戰船...。

（註：在遊戲初，是三國鼎立的局面，但到了前段中後，艾斯弗斯特還突然滅掉了格林堡王國，並殺死該國國王和大王子。此舉也導致，二王子逃亡，而僅剩艾斯弗斯特公國和聖海桑德大教國的局面。但艾斯弗斯特併吞格林堡後過於強大，主角僅剩一個小軍隊。此時幾乎只會選擇與聖海桑德大教國結盟。）

But if you are choosing the Frederica route, moral issues will rise up...it is morally questionable to use "the Aelfric"...as Serenoa and his team go deeper into the Ministry of Medicine to find the answer and wants to know what is the component of "the Aelfric"...and want to save the Roselle...they eventually find the book "*The Aelfric Method in Practice*", and are stunned to discover that "the Aelfric" is made from human remains of the Rosellan. They soon get caught by Lyla...and that's when their battle starts...as the head of the Ministry...Lyla has no choice but to guard the secret...

但如果你選擇了芙德麗卡路線，道德議題會浮現...使用「艾弗里克」會是具有道德爭議的事...尤其當瑟雷諾亞和他的團隊深入醫法院去查明真相，且想要知道「艾弗里克」的組成時...並且要拯救羅潔爾族時...他們最終發現了一本書《艾弗里克的運用法門》，並意外得知艾弗里克是由羅潔爾族的遺體所製成。他們被萊拉逮個正著...而這就是他們開始戰鬥的時候...身為醫法院的首腦...萊拉別無選擇地要守護這個秘密...。

（註：多數的人第一次玩大多會選擇芙德麗卡路線，也就是主角老婆路線，因為主角老婆的族人，也就是羅潔爾族，在故事中遭受極大的迫害，不替自己老婆挺身而出，其實還蠻怪的。）

❶ evaluate 評價、給...估值

❷ slash 大幅度的削減

❸ cooperative 合作的

❹ scheme 計畫；方案

❺ formidable 難以克服的，難對付的

❻ detonate 使爆炸；使觸發

❼ warship 戰船

❽ component 零件；成分

❾ remains 剩餘（物）；遺體

❿ guard 保衛；保護

And if you are choosing the route of the true ending...what will happen...

You will find three characters that have been greatly linked with Lyla. Decimal, Corentin, Medina

而如果你選擇真結局路線的話...又會發生甚麼事情呢...。
你會發現有三個角色與萊拉大有關聯：電丸、柯蘭狄和梅迪娜

Decimal is abandoned by the itinerary merchant, and eventually kindly be taken in Serenoa's army...

電丸被旅行商人所遺棄，最終受到好意收留而加入了瑟雷諾亞軍隊...。

During the battle, Decimal will soon recognize that Lyla is his first master. He is designed by the team of Lyla...to which, Lyla coldly responds, initial samples should all be processed and discarded...why on earth that Decimal still remains...

在戰鬥期間，電丸立即察覺到萊拉是她第一個主人，其是由萊拉的團隊所設計出的機器人...對此，萊拉冷冷地回應，初期型的樣本都應該被處理且丟棄掉才對啊！...為什麼電丸還在...

What about Corentin?

In chapter 3, gamers are faced with the dilemma of choosing between going to Aesfrost or the Holy State of Hyzante...if you choose to go to the Holy State of Hyzante, then you will get Corentin...

那柯蘭狄呢？在第三章，玩家面臨的進退兩難的困境是要選擇前往聖海桑德大教國還是艾斯弗斯特公國...，如果你選擇前往聖海桑德大教國，那麼你會得到柯蘭狄。

Upon arriving the Holy State of Hyzante, you will soon find that the country has several issues that make you rethink about the true freedom of the citizens. Corentin, an ice magician, gets the approval by Lyla, and joins the army of the Serenoa...now it is quite awkward to have a battle with Lyla, whom Corentin respects...deeply...

在抵達聖海桑德大教國時，你會立即發現國家有幾個議題讓你重新思考著關於人民的真自由這項議題。柯蘭狄是位冰魔法師，在萊拉的獲准之下加入了瑟雷諾亞的軍隊...現在相當尷尬的是，要與柯蘭狄深深敬重的萊拉閣下進行戰鬥...

（註：聖海桑德大教國並沒有想像中的美好，甚至思想受到侷限。在女神教主義的盛行下，人們甚至不能表達意見。教國也迫害羅潔爾族，讓羅潔爾族世代為奴。遊戲初，柯蘭狄就是因為察覺到這點，加上後來協助剿除叛黨有功，才獲准加入主角軍隊，離開聖海桑德大教國。）

Corentin mentions several facts. Ideas in the Holy State of Hyzante will inhibit one's thoughts, therefore, degenerating one's growth. So a great magician like Lyla should totally get rid of this...to which Lyla replies...unable to keep you on the team is such a regret.

柯蘭狄提到了幾項事實。在聖海桑德大教國的想法，會限制每個人民的思考，因此使個人成長有所退化。所以一個像萊拉這樣偉大的魔法師應該要全然放掉這些侷限...對此，萊拉回覆...無法留住你在我們的團隊是如此的損失。

❶ abandon 丟棄；拋棄

❷ itinerary merchant 旅行商人

❸ recognize 認出，識別

❹ discard 拋棄，丟棄

❺ dilemma 困境，進退兩難

❻ freedom 自由

❼ magician 魔術師，巫師

❽ approval 贊成；同意

❾ inhibit 禁止；約束；抑制

❿ degenerate 衰退；墮落

What about Medina? An aspiring apothecary who used to be a

trainee at the Ministry of Medicine...who eventually couldn't endure what she saw at the hospital, and embarked on what is actually right by joining the army of the Serenoa...

那梅迪娜呢?一個滿懷熱忱的藥劑師,過去曾在醫法院當實習生...其最終無法忍受在醫院所目睹到的事情,而展開了一趟旅程,加入了瑟雷諾亞軍隊以證明什麼才是對的...

(註:梅迪娜算是醫學院的學生,但是在實習時發現有許多事情不合理。她就如同剛出社會的新鮮人一般,但許多事情只能照醫法院的規定。不是每個病人她都能發揮所長並進行救治等等的。這也促成她的離開。她也因為這些事被萊拉酸過於天真。)

Till now, she still cannot understand what Lyla told her before...to be outspoken in front of Lyla that...after joining the army of the Serenoa...she understands that one has to trust what he or she believes in...this is also the way to convince himself or herself to move forward...

至今,她仍無法了解當初萊拉告訴她的那段話...在萊拉面前如此直言不諱...在加入瑟雷諾亞軍隊後...她了解到一個人必須要相信自己所相信的...這也是一個説服自己前進的一種方式...。

To which, Lyla indifferently responds, as a person who used to be the student of the Ministry of Medicine...yet still quite naïve...she totally admires courage, but she won't be lenient...and she won't...

　對此，萊拉冷漠地回應，一位過去曾是醫法院的學生…卻仍如此天真爛漫…她全然欽佩梅迪娜的勇氣，但是她不會手下留情…而她真的不會…

Lyla has the magic that can stop character's movement for several rounds, so that's why we mention earlier that even if you get Avlora…she can still make Avlora stop for several rounds, meaning having Avlora equals not having her…ha ha…

　萊拉有個魔法能夠讓角色停止活動幾個回合，所以這也是我們早先所描述到的，即使你得到艾芙蘿拉…萊拉仍可以讓艾芙蘿拉有幾回合無法行動。意謂著有艾芙蘿拉等同於沒有一樣…哈哈。

- 第 **21** 題，Despite previous acquaintance, one will act stringently，對應到 she totally admires courage, but she won't be lenient...and she won't...，act stringently = won't be lenient，故答案要選 **H** Minister Lyla。

- 第 **22** 題，With formidable skills in battle, one's join still cannot make the journey smooth，對應到 Lyla has the magic that can stop character's movement for several rounds 和 she can still make Avlora stop for several rounds, meaning having Avlora equals not having her...和 but if you think having the greatest warrior like Avlora, your road to beat one of the final battles with Minister Lyla will be smooth, then you are completely mistaken...，包含三句聽力訊息，但都指向有艾芙蘿拉的加入也無法讓後面的戰鬥一帆風順，故答案要選 **B** Avlora。

- 第 **23** 題，One's abandonment eventually gets compensated，對應到 Decimal is abandoned by the itinerary merchant, and eventually kindly be taken in Serenoa's army...，gets compensated = be taken in Serenoa's army...，電丸被聖海桑德大教國的醫法院丟棄後，又被旅行商人遺棄，因為覺得他常出錯又賣不到好價錢，但最後仍被好心的瑟雷諾亞收留，所以也算是種補償了，故答案要選 **E** Decimal。

● 第 **24** 題，Realization of the constraint of staying in a particular country，對應到 Corentin mentions several facts. Ideas in the Holy State of Hyzante will inhibit one's thoughts, therefore, degenerating one's growth. So a great magician like Lyla should totally get rid of this...，inhibit 對應到 constraint，指的就是待在聖海桑德大教國限制了一個人的思考和成長，故答案要選 **D** Corentin。

● 第 **25** 題，One's confidence in himself or herself plays a role in how one gets ahead，對應到 she understands that one has to trust what he or she believes in...this is also the way to convince himself or herself to move forward...，confidence = believes in，指要對自己有信念才能大步往前邁進，故答案要選 **C** Medina。

● 第 **26** 題，Seeking the truth behind what is the component of "the Aelfric"，對應到 But if you are choosing the Frederica route, moral issues will rise up...it is morally questionable to use "the Aelfric"...as Serenoa and his team go deeper into the Ministry of Medicine to find the answer，選擇此路線會遇到道德問題，也才會有找尋真相，找尋真相也就是 it is morally questionable to use "the Aelfric"，故答案要選 **J** a Frederica route。

● 第 **27** 題，Plays a weighty role in exploding the warship of the Aesfrost，對應到 gamers have to defeat all Aesfrost forces and then use the formidable substance to detonate the warship of the Aesfrost...and why do we talk about the substance...because it is relevant to one of the battles with Lyla...the formidable substance is purple, and is called "the Aelfric"，Plays a weighty role = the formidable substance to detonate the warship，要毀掉戰船，關鍵就是埃弗里克，故答案要選 **F** the Aelfric。

● **第 28 題**，Involves the method of manufacturing a material，對應到 they eventually find the book "the Aelfric Method in Practice", and are stunned to discover that "the Aelfric" is made from human remains of the Rosellan，要在醫法院找到這本書，才能得知是如何製造的，以及得知原來成分是利用羅潔爾族的屍體，很慘無人道，故答案要選 **I** *The Aelfric Method in Practice*。

● **第 29 題**，The greatest warrior will be added to your team，對應到 And if you meet all the criteria for the true ending, you will get Avlora in chapter 17...，前面有講到 Avlora 的能力多強，The greatest warrior = Avlora，get Avlora = will be added to your team，但是加入條件是，玩家要達到真結局的條件，故答案要選 **K** the true ending route。

● **第 30 題**，Whose magic involves immobilization that can greatly slash down the team's mobility，對應到 Lyla has the magic that can stop character's movement for several rounds，immobilization = stop，stop character's movement for several rounds = greatly slash down the team's mobility，故答案要選 **H** Minister Lyla。

▶▶ 填空測驗

| Instruction | MP3 011

　　現在請再聽一次音檔，並做下列的測驗，檢視自己能否完成此填空測驗和強化自己聽力能力和拼字能力，降低並修正自己漏聽到聽力訊息的機會，大幅提升應考實力。

　　There are several formidable **1.**＿＿＿＿＿＿ throughout the game, Triangle Strategy, even if you are not playing hard mode. Gamers choosing "normal" still find themselves having a hard time in key battles, especially in chapter 7, *Not a Word, My Friend*. Players are stuck with having in a war with one of the greatest **2.**＿＿＿＿＿＿, Avlora, the awesome female fighter, whose attack can slash most characters' 70% to 80% HP, making most **3.**＿＿＿＿＿ to have a flight with her **4.**＿＿＿＿＿, and almost all characters cannot endure her attack twice...during the battle with Avlora, not using the **5.**＿＿＿＿＿ trap to win the game presents a great challenge for most gamers even under "normal" by using only 10 **6.**＿＿＿＿＿...however, we are not talking about Avlora today, since she has garnered too much of the **7.**＿＿＿＿＿＿ from most players...if so who shall we be talking to...

　　To be honest, most gamers will play this game for more than one round, and actually there are five endings throughout the game...however, only one of them will be the true ending. In two of these endings...near the very end, you are bound to encounter Minister Lyla, the **8.**＿＿＿＿＿, with the ability that you cannot take it too **9.**＿＿＿＿＿...

And if you meet all the criteria for the true ending, you will get Avlora in chapter 17, but if you think having the greatest warrior like Avlora, your road to beat one of the final battles with Minister Lyla will be **10.**_____, then you are completely mistaken......

Under two **11.**_____, you will have a fight with Lyla. The first one is choosing a Frederica route, and the second one is the true ending route...

During these routes, players will still have to go through several scenes that will require them to **12.**_____ their relationships with Aesfrost and the Holy State of Hyzante...there are no right or wrong answers...just considerations for the benefit of the country...

In the middle part of the game, most will get an ally with the Holy State of Hyzante to slash down the power of Aesfrost...that will include another three choices...simply put, in one of the **13.**_____ schemes with the Holy State of Hyzante, gamers have to defeat all Aesfrost forces and then use the formidable substance to **14.**_____ the warship of the Aesfrost...and why do we talk about the substance...because it is relevant to one of the battles with Lyla...the formidable substance is **15.**_____, and is called "the Aelfric"...at that time, we can only know it's powerful enough to destroy the **16.**_____ of the Aesfrost...

But if you are choosing the Frederica route, moral issues will rise up...it is morally questionable to use "the Aelfric"...as Serenoa and his team go deeper into the Ministry of Medicine to find the answer and wants to know what is the **17.**_____ of "the Aelfric"...and want to save the Roselle...they eventually find the book "the Aelfric Method in Practice", and are stunned to discover that "the Aelfric" is made from human **18.**_____ of the Rosellan. They soon get caught by Lyla...and that's when their battle starts...as the head of the Ministry...Lyla has no choice but to guard the **19.**_____...And if you are choosing the route of the true ending...what will happen...You will find three characters that have been greatly linked with Lyla. Decimal, Corentin, Medina

Decimal is abandoned by the itinerary **20.**_____, and eventually kindly be taken in Serenoa's army...During the battle, Decimal will soon recognize that Lyla is his first master. He is designed by the team of Lyla...to which, Lyla coldly responds, initial **21.**_____ should all be processed and discarded...why on earth that Decimal still remains...

Upon arriving the Holy State of Hyzante, you will soon find that the country has several issues that make you rethink about the true freedom of the **22.**_____. Corentin, an **23.**_____ magician, gets the approval by Lyla, and joins the army of the Serenoa...now it is quite awkward to have a battle with Lyla, whom Corentin respects...deeply...

Corentin mentions several facts. Ideas in the Holy State of Hyzante will inhibit one's thoughts, therefore, **24.**_____ one's

Test 1

Test 2

Test 3

Test 4

growth. So a great **25.**＿＿＿＿＿＿ like Lyla should totally get rid of this...to which Lyla replies...unable to keep you on the team is such a regret. What about Medina? An aspiring **26.**＿＿＿＿＿＿ who used to be a trainee at the Ministry of Medicine...who eventually couldn't endure what she saw at the hospital, and embarked on what is actually right by joining the army of the Serenoa...Till now, she still cannot understand what Lyla told her before...to be **27.**＿＿＿＿＿＿ in front of Lyla that...after joining the army of the Serenoa...she understands that one has to trust what he or she believes in...this is also the way to convince himself or herself to move forward...

To which, Lyla indifferently responds, as a person who used to be the student of the Ministry of Medicine...yet still quite naïve...she totally admires **28.**＿＿＿＿＿, but she won't be lenient...and she won't...Lyla has the **29.**＿＿＿＿＿＿ that can stop character's movement for several rounds, so that's why we mention earlier that even if you get Avlora...she can still make Avlora stop for several rounds, meaning having Avlora **30.**＿＿＿＿＿＿ not having her...ha ha...

| 參考答案 |

1. skirmishes
2. warriors
3. discouraging
4. head-on
5. fire
6. units
7. limelight
8. sorceress
9. lightly
10. smooth
11. circumstances
12. evaluate
13. cooperative
14. detonate
15. purple
16. warship
17. component
18. remains
19. secret
20. merchant
21. samples
22. citizens
23. ice
24. degenerating
25. magician
26. apothecary
27. outspoken
28. courage
29. magic
30. equals

Section 4
Questions 31-40

Write the correct letter, A-N, next to Questions 31-40

A Gustadolph

B Dragan

C *The Power of Salt*

D Serenoa

E Thalas

F Svarog

G Prince Roland

H Frederica

I the Grand Norzelian Mines

J Aesfrost

K Glenbrook

L the Holy State of Hyzante

M Prince Roland and Serenoa

N pink rocks

31. Important elements discovered at the cavern
32. Conduct underhanded plans to the shipment of goods
33. Has something valuable for the negotiation with two nations
34. The schemer behind the assassination
35. Return to the nation because of the imminent danger
36. Previous smart moves come back to bite him
37. One's acknowledgment that something is of vital value
38. Desire to be dominant among three nations
39. Overturn the situation during the discussion
40. Is given a mission to supervise an important site

Test 1

Test 2

Test 3

Test 4

影子跟讀練習 MP3 012

做完題目後，除了對答案知道錯的部分在哪外，更重要的是要修正自己聽力根本的問題，即聽力理解力和聽力專注力，聽力專注力的修正能逐步強化本身的聽力實力，所以現在請根據聽力內容「逐個段落」、「數個段落」或「整篇」進行跟讀練習，提升在實際考場時專注聽完每個訊息、定位出關鍵考點和搭配筆記回答完所有題目。Go!

In chapter 10, gamers choosing the route of surreptitiously transporting salt to Aesfrost will be surprised to learn that the schemer is actually Svarog, Frederica's uncle. He is also the father of Dragan...

在第 10 章，玩家選擇秘密地將鹽運送到艾斯弗斯特公國的話，會因為幕後的策畫人是斯瓦羅格，也就是芙德麗卡的叔叔，而大吃一驚。斯瓦羅格也是德蘭格的父親。

And why are we paying so much attention on Dragan...rather than discussing either Frederica or Svarog...because there is a conspiracy behind Dragan's death...that is also the reason why Svarog remains doubtful on everything happening these days...and who killed his son...

那我們又為何要將那麼多的焦點放在德蘭格呢...而不是討論芙德麗卡或斯瓦羅格呢...因為德蘭格的死其背後是有個陰謀在的...那也是為什麼斯瓦羅格對於那些日子所發生的每件事情都抱持懷疑...還有到底是誰殺害他兒子的...

This also presents a dilemma for all gamers...how to make Svarog believe in them...definitely not something trivial...

這也對所有玩家造成進退兩難的困境...要如何取信斯瓦羅格呢...當然不可能會是些雞毛蒜皮的瑣事...。

The main character Serenoa eventually is given with two options. First, not to disclose Prince Roland's real identity and then have a negotiation with Svarog.

主角瑟雷諾亞最終有兩個選擇。第一個是不揭露羅蘭王子的真實身分，然後與斯瓦羅格協商。

Second, boldly tell Svarog the truth that Prince Roland's alive... Since Serenoa has to protect Prince Roland...there are certainly lots of pros and cons...if players want to reveal Roland's real identity...

第二是，大膽地告訴斯瓦羅格真相，羅蘭王子還活著...。
既然瑟雷諾亞必須要保護羅蘭王子...確實有許多利弊要考量...如果玩家選擇要揭露羅蘭王子的真實身分。

Even though Serenoa knows the real killer...directly pointing the gun at the killer won't be of much help...and we do have to know what happened before...

儘管瑟雷諾亞知道真正的兇手是誰...直接指出真兇並沒有太大的幫助...而且我們必須要了解先前到底發生了什麼事情...。

That's why we have to go way back to chapter 4...

In chapter 4, players are given a mission to protect Dragan from Aesfrost's soldiers...

這也就是為什麼我們要回到早先的第四章...。

在第四章，玩家被賦予一項任務就是保護德蘭格免於艾斯弗斯特軍的攻擊...。

❶ surreptitiously 祕密地；暗中地
❷ transport 運送
❸ conspiracy 陰謀
❹ doubtful 懷疑的
❺ trivial 瑣細的；不重要的
❻ real identity 真實身分
❼ negotiation 協商
❽ reveal 揭露

All things result from the job given by King Glenbrook to his son Prince Roland and for Roland to oversee the Grand Norzelian Mines and reward those miners at the site...Dragan is the person in charge at the site and who happens to find something of great importance...that can totally give him an upper hand when it comes to the negotiation with Gustadolph, who is the archduke of Aesfrost...

所有的事情都導因於格林堡國王給予他兒子羅蘭王子的任務，也就是要羅蘭去巡視新諾澤利亞礦山並且獎勵在礦山的挖礦工人...德蘭格則是在該礦山的主導人，也是碰巧發現了重大發現的人...這絕對讓他獲取了與古斯塔德弗，也就是艾斯弗斯特公國的主帥的協商時占有優勢...。

The unified exploitation is effort made by three nations, Aesfrost, Glenbrook, and the Holy State of Hyzante...it has to be mutually shared...

聯合開採是由三個國家的共同努力：艾斯弗斯特公國、格林堡王國和聖海桑德大教國...所以開採物是必須要共享的...。

However, Dragan thinks of something too emboldened...that he can transcend his father Svarog and Gustadolph...does he bite off more than he can chew?

然而，德蘭格的想法卻更為大膽包天...他可以超越自己父親斯瓦羅格和古斯塔德弗...他這樣做會是不自量力嗎？

Even Gustadolph admits in front of his brother Thalas that things discovered is too valuable...

即使古斯塔德弗在自己弟弟塔拉斯面前，都坦承了所發現的東西價值連城...。

Dragan wants to use this great information as a way for him to get the position of prime minister of Aesfrost...and it is precious enough to equate the title with the things discovered...the question is does Gustadolph see things in the same way...?

德蘭格想要用這麼棒的訊息作為讓自己獲取艾斯弗斯特公國首相的職位...而卻是所發現之物珍貴到足以與這個頭銜的價值並駕齊驅...問題是古斯塔德弗也是這樣想的嗎...？

Dragan informs of all miners that things should be kept secretly and handed them over exclusively to Aesfrost...then Dragan writes a letter to Gustadolph, threatening him that if he does not comply with naming him the prime minister of Aesfrost, he will go directly to Glenbrook...that is what Dragan gleefully tells all the miners that he will soon be either the prime minister of Aesfrost or the ambassador of Glenbrook...

德蘭格告知所有挖礦者，發現的東西必須要保密，並且僅能由艾斯弗斯特公國獨佔並交給該國...緊接著，德蘭格寫了封信給古斯塔德弗，威脅他，如果他不順從，並且任命他為艾斯弗斯特公國的首相的話，那麼他會直接改與格林堡王國交涉...這也是德蘭格興高采烈地告訴所有挖礦工人，他可能即將成為艾斯弗斯特公國的首相或者是格林堡王國的大使...。

❶ reward 報答，報償
❷ importance 重要，重大
❸ exploitation 開發；開採
❹ effort 努力
❺ embolden 使大膽；使有勇氣
❻ transcend 超越；優於
❼ valuable 值錢的，貴重的
❽ information 消息；資訊
❾ precious 貴重的，寶貴的

❿ equate 等同

To complete the mission, gamers have to protect Dragan from Aesfrost's soldiers...but sadly, Dragan will still get killed eventually...by one of Aesfrost's bowmen...

為了完成這項任務，玩家要保護德蘭格免受艾斯弗斯特公國的攻擊...但令人感到悲傷的是，德蘭格最終仍會被...艾斯弗斯特公國其中一位弓箭手殺死...。

And right before the incident, during the conversation between Thalas and Gustadolph, Thalas tells his brother that he will take care of it...that includes getting rid of Dragan's carcass. There is even an attack launched by Aesfrost to Glenbrook, so Prince Roland and Serenoa have no choice but to go back to Glenbrook immediately, so Thalas has the time to do the dirty work after Dragan's death...

在這事件發生之前，在塔拉斯和古斯塔德弗的談話中，塔拉斯告訴他哥哥，他會將一切都處理好的...這包含了除掉德蘭格的屍體。甚至在事件發生後，艾斯弗斯特公國對格林堡王國發動攻擊，所以羅蘭王子和瑟雷諾亞別無選擇地要即刻回到格林堡王國，所以在德蘭格死掉後，塔拉斯有時間去執行他的骯髒活...。

Gustadolph certainly wants a monopoly, so even if giving the title to Dragan means little to him, he just doesn't want to be menaced and wants to be the king among three nations.

古斯塔德弗確實想要獨佔，所以即使給德蘭格頭銜對他來說也沒什麼意義，他不想要被人威脅，且他想要成為三個國家中的王。

But is killing Dragan a smart move? Or that simply tells us the stupidity of Dragan...? Let's not jump to the conclusion quickly...

但是，殺掉德蘭格是古斯塔德弗聰明之舉嗎？或者這僅告訴了我們德蘭格的愚蠢...？讓我們飛快跳到結尾...。

Remember we have talked about rewarding those miners....? In exchange, Dragan gives a book, named *The Power of Salt*, to Serenoa.

記得，我們提到過要獎勵那些礦工嗎...？德蘭格贈與瑟雷諾亞一本書《鹽中所蘊含的力量》。

The book will be a powerful tool when it comes to the negotiation with Gustadolph at the very end of the story...making Gustadolph regret of having Dragan killed...and one more thing... what does Dragan find at the end of the tunnel that is valuable for him to get the position of the prime minister...

在非常接近故事結尾，與古斯塔德弗交涉時，這本書成了強而有力的法寶...讓古斯塔德弗後悔殺死德蘭格...而還有一件事情...德蘭格在隧道末端到底是發現了什麼，有價值連城到能夠替他換取首相的職位...。

It's actually pink rocks or salt crystals...things that the Holy State has been looking for also...I guess that's the end of the today's class...

實際上，所發現的是粉紅色岩石或岩鹽...聖海桑德大教國也一直在找尋的東西...我想今天的課堂就到此結束了...。

❶ bowmen 弓箭手

❷ incident 事件；插曲

❸ carcass（動物的）屍體

❹ monopoly 獨佔

❺ menace 威脅，恐嚇

❻ stupidity 愚蠢，愚笨

❼ miners 礦工

❽ regret 懊悔

❾ tunnel 隧道

❿ valuable 值錢的，貴重的

● **第 31 題**，Important elements discovered at the cavern，對應到 what does Dragan find at the end of the tunnel that is valuable for him to get the position of the prime minister...和 It's actually pink rocks or salt crystals...things that the Holy State has been looking for also，cavern = tunnel，所發現的重要且關鍵性的物質，就是粉紅色岩石或岩鹽，故答案要選 **N** pink rocks。

● **第 32 題**，Conduct underhanded plans to the shipment of goods，對應到 gamers choosing the route of surreptitiously transporting salt to Aesfrost will be surprised to find that the schemer is actually Svarog, Frederica's uncle，shipment = transporting，underhanded plans = surreptitiously 和 schemer，故答案要選 **F** Svarog。

● **第 33 題**，Has something valuable for the negotiation with two nations，對應到 Dragan wants to use this great information as a way for him to get the position of prime minister of Aesfrost...and it is precious enough to equate the title with the things discovered...，the negotiation with two nations 指的就是，Dragan 能夠分別用這個有價值的東西跟格林堡和艾斯佛斯特兩國談判以換取他想要的職位，故答案要選 **B** Dragan。

● **第 34 題**，The schemer behind the assassination，對應到 And right before the incident, during the conversation between Thalas and

Gustadolph, Thalas tells his brother that he will take care of it...that includes getting rid of Dragan's carcass. ，Thalas 說 will take care of it，所以他才是暗殺德蘭格的幕後人，故答案要選 **E** Thalas。

- 第 **35** 題，Return to the nation because of the imminent danger，對應到 Prince Roland and Serenoa have no choice but to go back to Glenbrook immediately，have no choice but to go back = because of the imminent danger，因為格林堡突然被攻打，有迫近的危險，他們只能先回到自己國家，暫時無法管德蘭格的事情了，故答案要選 **M** Prince Roland and Serenoa。

- 第 **36** 題，Previous smart moves come back to bite him，對應到 The book will be a powerful tool when it comes to the negotiation with Gustadolph at the very end of the story...making Gustadolph regret of having Dragan killed... ，Gustadolph 的後悔，證明了先前殺害德蘭格不是 smart move，儘管先前他認為是，而殺害德蘭格反而之後讓他在和瑟雷諾亞談判時失去優勢，因為德蘭格有將書交給瑟雷諾亞，書中的資料能讓 Gustadolph 不得不同意談判，這點也是他之前想不到的，故答案要選 **A** Gustadolph。

- 第 **37** 題，One's acknowledgment that something is of vital value，對應到 Even Gustadolph admits in front of his brother Thalas that things discovered is too valuable... ，acknowledgment = admits，故答案要選 **A** Gustadolph。

- 第 **38** 題，Desire to be dominant among three nations，對應到 Gustadolph certainly wants a monopoly, so even if giving the title to Dragan means little to him, he just doesn't want to be menaced and wants to be the king among three nations，the king among three nations = dominant among three nations，故答案要選 **A** Gustadolph。

- 第 **39** 題，Overturn the situation during the discussion，對應到 The book will be a powerful tool when it comes to the negotiation with Gustadolph at the very end of the story...making Gustadolph regret of having Dragan killed，Overturn the situation = The book will be a powerful tool，故答案要選 **C** *The Power of Salt*。

- 第 **40** 題，Is given a mission to supervise an important site，對應到 All things result from the job given by King of Glenbrook to his son Prince Roland and for Roland to oversee the Grand Norzelian Mines and reward those miners at the site...，given a mission to supervise = the job given by King of Glenbrook to his son Prince Roland and for Roland to oversee，故答案要選 **G** Prince Roland。

▶▶ 填空測驗

| Instruction | MP3 012

現在請再聽一次音檔，並做下列的測驗，檢視自己能否完成此填空測驗和強化自己聽力能力和拼字能力，降低並修正自己漏聽到聽力訊息的機會，大幅提升應考實力。

In chapter 10, gamers choosing the route of **1.**_____ transporting salt to Aesfrost will be surprised to find that the schemer is actually Svarog, Frederica's uncle... And why are we paying so much attention on Dragan...rather than discussing either Frederica or Svarog...because there is a **2.**_____ behind Dragan's **3.**_____ _____...that is also the reason why Svarog remains doubtful on everything happening these days...and who killed his son...

This also presents a **4.**_____ for all gamers...how to make Svarog believe in them...definitely not something trivial...The main character Serenoa eventually is given with two **5.**_____. First, not to disclose Prince Roland's real identity and then have a negotiation with Svarog

Second, boldly tell Svarog the truth that Prince Roland's alive...Since Serenoa has to protect Prince Roland...there are certainly lots of pros and cons...if players want to reveal Roland's real **6.**_____ _____...

Even though Serenoa knows the **7.**_____ killer...directly

pointing the gun at the killer won't be of much help...and we do have to know what happened before...That's why we have to go way back to chapter 4...In chapter 4, players are given a **8.**_____ to protect Dragan from Aesfrost's soldiers...

All things result from the job given by King Glenbrook to his son Prince Roland and for Roland to **9.**_____ the Grand Norzelian Mines and reward those **10.**_____ at the site...Dragan is the person in charge at the site and who happens to find something of great importance...that can totally give him an upper hand when it comes to the negotiation with Gustadolph, who is the **11.**_____ of Aesfrost...

The unified **12.**_____ is effort made by three nations, Aesfrost, Glenbrook, and the Holy State of Hyzante...it has to be mutually shared...However, Dragan thinks of something too **13.**_____ _____...that he can **14.**_____ his father Svarog and Gustadolph...does he bite off more than he can chew?

Dragan wants to use this great **15.**_____ as a way for him to get the position of prime minister of Aesfrost...and it is precious enough to **16.**_____ the title with the things discovered...the question is does Gustadolph see things in the same way...?

Dragan informs of all miners that things should be kept secretly and handed them over **17.**_____ to Aesfrost...then Dragan writes a letter to Gustadolph, **18.**_____ him that if he does not comply with naming him the prime minister of Aesfrost, he will go directly to Glenbrook...that is what Dragan gleefully tells all the miners that he will soon be either the prime minister of Aesfrost or the **19.**＿＿＿＿＿＿ of Glenbrook...

To complete the mission, gamers have to protect Dragan from Aesfrost's **20.**＿＿＿＿＿＿...but sadly, Dragan will still get killed eventually...by one of Aesfrost's **21.**＿＿＿＿＿＿...And right before the incident, during the conversation between Thalas and Gustadolph, Thalas tells his brother that he will take care of it...that includes getting rid of Dragan's **22.**＿＿＿＿＿＿. There is even an attack launched by Aesfrost to Glenbrook, so Prince Roland and Serenoa have no choice but to go back to Glenbrook immediately, so Thalas has the time to do the dirty work after Dragan's death...

Gustadolph certainly wants a **23.**＿＿＿＿＿＿, so even if giving the title to Dragan means little to him, he just doesn't want to be **24.**＿＿ ＿＿＿＿＿＿ and wants to be the king among three nations.

But is killing Dragan a **25.**＿＿＿＿＿＿ move? Or that simply tells us the **26.**＿＿＿＿＿＿ of Dragan...? Let's not jump to the conclusion quickly...Remember we have talked about rewarding those miners....? In exchange, Dragan gives a book, named *The Power of Salt*, to Serenoa.

The book will be a powerful tool when it comes to the negotiation with Gustadolph at the very end of the story...making Gustadolph **27.**＿＿＿＿＿＿ of having Dragan killed...and one more thing... what does Dragan find at the end of the tunnel that is valuable for him to get the position of the prime **28.**_____...It's actually **29.**_____ rocks or **30.**_____ crystals...things that the Holy State has been looking for also...I guess that's the end of the today's class...

參考答案

1. surreptitiously	**2.** conspiracy
3. death	**4.** dilemma
5. options	**6.** identity
7. real	**8.** mission
9. oversee	**10.** miners
11. archduke	**12.** exploitation
13. emboldened	**14.** transcend
15. information	**16.** equate
17. exclusively	**18.** threatening
19. ambassador	**20.** soldiers
21. bowmen	**22.** carcass
23. monopoly	**24.** menaced
25. smart	**26.** stupidity
27. regret	**28.** minister
29. pink	**30.** salt

Complete the Notes below

Write NO MORE THAN TWO WORDS for each answer

- The waiter has the **1.**_____ of the room, so he gets to dim the light from outside.
- Obscuring the light actually helps because spiders have a **2.**_____.
- They don't care about these spiders on the bed if they stay **3.**_____.
- To fix the lock and open the door, the waiter has to get the **4.**_____.
- Spider's **5.**_____ will be hindered by dance movement, according to the waiter.

- Spiders are afraid of the **6.**＿＿＿＿＿ from the vase.
- Spiders do get smaller, but sprinkling water onto them make the quit and pillow all wet.
- It is often assumed that the ring will bring bad luck.
- There is an immediate fire right after, so they have to get the fire **7.**＿＿＿＿＿.
- The waiter has got some **8.**＿＿＿＿＿, so he needs some pills.
- They do need to retreat to the secret passage because of the fire.
- One of them is immune to carbon monoxide, so still has the mood to take **9.**＿＿＿＿＿ and **10.**＿＿＿＿＿ during the retreat.

- **第 1 題**，The waiter has the **1.**_____ of the room, so he gets to dim the light from outside，對應到 Then I'm dimming the light...等等，但是要注意試題較考驗整合能力，且聽力訊息是到聽到第三題答案後，A 表明因為自己有 remote control，故可以從外面控制燈光明暗，故答案為 **remote control**。

- **第 2 題**，Obscuring the light actually helps because spiders have a **2.**_____，對應到 they have a **poor eyesight**...obscuring the light actually helps you guys...，they 指的就是 spiders，故答案為 **poor eyesight**。

- **第 3 題**，They don't care about these spiders on the bed if they stay **3.**_____，對應到 I don't even mind their occupying our bed...as long as they remain **docile**...，故答案為 **docile**。

- **第 4 題**，To fix the lock and open the door, the waiter has to get the **4.**_____，對應到 let me get my **toolbox**...，在 B 詢問後，A 回答要去取工具箱，故答案為 **toolbox**。

- **第 5 題**，Spider's **5.**_____ will be hindered by dance movement, according to the waiter，對應到 but dance movement actually confuses those spiders...It influences their **visual** perception，confuse 和 influence 整合成 be hindered，故答案為 **visual perception**。

- **第 6 題**，Spiders are afraid of the **6.** _____ from the vase，對應到 I think they are afraid of the **fragrance** coming from the vase...I'm spreading the water onto them（要耐心聽到更後面的訊息），故答案為 **fragrance**。

- **第 7 題**，There is an immediate fire right after, so they have to get the fire **7.** _____，對應到 There is a fire in the corridor. Go get the fire **extinguisher**...（這題也是有進行改寫，要整合句意），故答案為 **extinguisher**。

- **第 8 題**，The waiter has got some **8.** _____, so he needs some pills，對應到 I've got some **migraine**...Can I trouble you with some pills，故答案為 **migraine**。

- **第 9 題**，One of them is immune to carbon monoxide, so still has the mood to take **9.** _____ and **10.** _____ during the retreat，對應到 Fine, I'm taking two adorable **coffee mugs** next to the desk lamp with me...，故答案為 **coffee mugs**。

- **第 10 題**，One of them is immune to carbon monoxide, so still has the mood to take **9.**＿＿＿＿＿ and **10.**＿＿＿＿＿ during the retreat，對應到 I'm going to take this **elephant plate** as well...（這題較難，需要一直聽到最後才出現，聽力訊息並未一開始就說明要帶哪兩種東西走），故答案為 **elephant plate**。

影子跟讀練習 MP3 013

做完題目後，除了對答案知道錯的部分在哪外，更重要的是要修正自己聽力根本的問題，即聽力理解力和聽力專注力，聽力專注力的修正能逐步強化本身的聽力實力，所以現在請根據聽力內容「逐個段落」、「數個段落」或「整篇」進行跟讀練習，提升在實際考場時專注聽完每個訊息、定位出關鍵考點和搭配筆記回答完所有題目。**Go!**

| B |

The crucifix won't work...

| B |

十字架起不了作用...

| A |

Then I'm dimming the light..?

| A |

那麼我把燈調暗...？

| B |

Why? And from outside? Too make us feel more worrisome? Having two tremendous spiders in the room is bad enough already.

| B |

為什麼要這麼做？從外頭可以？讓我們的擔憂更甚嗎？房間裡有兩隻巨型蜘蛛已經夠糟了。

| C |

I don't even mind their occupying our bed...as long as they remain **docile**...

| C |

我甚至不介意牠們佔據我們的床...只要牠們保持溫馴...

| A |

I have the **remote control** of the room...so from outside...and they have a **poor eyesight**...obscuring the light actually helps you guys...

| A |

我有房間的遠端遙控...所以從外頭可以...而且蜘蛛的視力不良...將光模糊化實際上對你們有助益...。

| B |

by the way, can you fix the lock and open the door...

| B |

附帶一提的是，你可以修復門鎖然後把房門打開嗎？

| A |

let me get my **toolbox**...I am sure I will be in time to save you...or not...but dance movement actually confuses those spiders...It influences their **visual perception**.

| **A** |

讓我去拿我的工具箱...我確信我會及時來救你們...也可能是來不及...但是跳舞的律動實際上會讓那些蜘蛛感到困惑...會影響蜘蛛的視覺感知。

| **C** |

like the trick male jumping spiders do to the females?...it wouldn't hurt to give it a try...if they attack..

| **C** |

就像雄性跳蛛對雌性跳蛛所做的伎倆嗎？如果牠們攻擊的話，試試看無妨...。

| **B** |

How about something bolder...sprinkle the water from the vase...?

| **B** |

要試試看更大膽的方法嗎？...撒些花瓶裡的水呢...？

| **C** |

then you do it...where is this crazy thought coming from?

| **C** |

那你來潑灑吧！...這個瘋狂的想法是從哪冒出來的？

| **B** |

Don't move and stay right there...I think they are afraid of the **fragrance** coming from the vase...I'm spreading the water onto them...

| B |

別移動，停在那裡...我想牠們懼怕從花瓶裡傳出來的香氣...我正將花瓶內的水灑到牠們身上...。

| C |

They do shrink! It's like you are performing the magic show...but what about the quilt and the pillow...they are all wet...

| C |

蜘蛛真的縮小了！就像是你表演了一場魔法秀...但是被子和枕頭怎麼辦...都濕掉了...。

| B |

As long as we don't have to deal with the spiders anymore...I'm fine sleeping on the sofa...

| B |

只要我們不用再應付蜘蛛的話...睡在沙發上還可以接受的説。

| C |

Ok...and why does it take the guy so long to get the toolbox?

| C |

好...那為什麼那個人去拿工具箱要花這麼久的時間？

| B |

I don't know...oh...little moonlight from the window...

| B |

我不知道...噢！從窗戶外有些許月光透進來...

| C |

Who's out there? A guy with the ax?

| C |

誰在外頭？拿著斧頭的男人？

| B |

Why do we have to deal with one crisis after another? It's not the scary movie...I think I'm having a panic attack

| B |

為什麼我們要應付接連的危機呢？這又不是恐怖片...我想我的無端恐懼症要發作了

| A |

Are you guys ok? I bring some snack that's why it took me so long...and where are those spiders? You are not fabricating the story, are you?

| A |

你們還好嗎？我帶了些點心，這就是為什麼我去了這麼久...還有那些蜘蛛都去哪了？你們不是在編故事吧，是嗎？

| B |

I think they are gone after they have shrunk the size...did you see our friends?

| B |

我想牠們在察覺自己體型縮小後，就跑掉了...你有看到我們的朋友嗎？

| A |

No, I assumed they are with you guys in the room...oh...there is a ring on the floor...that's odd...it is often assumed that the ring will bring bad luck...

| A |

沒看到，我以為他們跟你們都待在房裡...噢！地板上有個戒指...還真怪...通常會認定這枚戒指會帶來不幸...。

| B |

like a sudden fire...?

| B |

像是突然起了火...？

| C |

Look! There is a fire in the corridor. Go get the fire **extinguisher**...

| C |

瞧！在走廊那裡起了火。去拿滅火器...。

| B |

Can we break the window?

| B |

我們可以打破窗戶嗎？

| C |

There might be a killer outside, and you would rather get axed than extinguish the fire...

| C |

外頭可能有個殺人犯，而你情願被斧頭砍死，也不願意去滅火...。

| A |

I've got some **migraine**...Can I trouble you with some pills?

| A |

我有些頭痛...可以跟你們討些藥丸嗎？

| B |

I have some herbs? And where is my bag?

| B |

我有些藥草...我的袋子去哪了呢？

| C |

I can't find mine, either...what should we do...the fire is getting increasingly fierce...

| C |

我也找不到我的袋子...我們該怎麼辦...火越來越猛烈了...。

| A |

break the window to get more air...then we go down to the secret passage

| A |

打破窗戶讓更多空氣進來...然後我們下去那條密道...

| B |

Fine, I'm taking two adorable **coffee mugs** next to the desk lamp with me...

| B |

好吧，那我要帶走在桌燈旁的兩個可愛的咖啡杯...。

| C |

Can we go now...I'm having a hard time breathing?

| C |

我們可以走了嗎？...我呼吸開始感到困難？

| B |

Perhaps the fragrance from the vase will cause someone ill under normal condition, but when the oxygen is scarce, your body functions better.

| B |

或許花瓶內的香氣讓人們在正常情況下感到不適，但是當氧氣缺乏時，你的身體變得更好了。

| A |

You're saying that you are immune to carbon monoxide?

| A |

你是在說，你對一氧化碳免疫了嗎？

| B |

I'm going to take this **elephant plate** as well...

| B |

我也要拿走這個大象的盤子...。

| Instruction | MP3 013

　　現在請再聽一次音檔，並做下列的測驗，檢視自己能否完成此填空測驗和強化自己聽力能力和拼字能力，降低並修正自己漏聽到聽力訊息的機會，大幅提升應考實力。

| B |

The crucifix won't work...

| A |

Then I'm dimming the light..?

| B |

Why? And from outside? Too make us feel more worrisome? Having two tremendous spiders in the room is bad enough already.

| C |

I don't even mind their occupying our bed...as long as they remain docile...

| A |

I have the remote **1.**_____ of the room...so from outside...and they have a poor **2.**_____...obscuring the **3.**_____ actually helps you guys...

| **B** |

by the way, can you fix the lock and open the door...

| **A** |

let me get my toolbox...I am sure I will be in time to save you...or not...but **4.**_____ movement actually confuses those spiders...It influences their visual **5.**_____

| **C** |

like the trick male **6.**_____ spiders do to the females?...it wouldn't hurt to give it a try...if they attack..

| **B** |

How about something bolder...**7.**_____ the water from the vase...?

| **C** |

then you do it...where is this crazy thought coming from?

| **B** |

Don't move and stay right there...I think they are afraid of the fragrance coming from the vase...I'm spreading the water onto them...

| **C** |

They do shrink! It's like you are performing the magic show...but what about the **8.**_____ and the **9.**_____...they are all wet...

| B |

As long as we don't have to deal with the spider anymore...I'm fine sleeping on the **10.**_____...

| C |

Ok...and why does it take the guy so long to get the toolbox?

| B |

I don't know...oh...little moonlight from the window...

| C |

Who's out there? A guy with the **11.**_____?

| B |

Why do we have to deal with one crisis after another? It's not the scary **12.**_____...I think I'm having a panic attack

| A |

Are you guys ok? I bring some **13.**_____ that why it took me so long...and where are those spiders? You are not **14.**_____ the story, are you?

| B |

I think they are gone after they have shrunk the size...did you see our friends?

| A |

No, I assumed they are with you guys in the room...oh...there is a ring on the floor...that's odd...it is often assumed that the ring will bring bad **15.**_____...

| B |

like a sudden fire...?

| C |

Look! There is a fire in the **16.**_____. Go get the fire **17.**__ _____...

| B |

Can we break the window?

| C |

There might be a killer outside, and you would rather get axed than **18.**_____ the fire...

| A |

I've got some **19.**_____...Can I trouble you with some **20.**_____?

| B |

I have some **21.**_____? And where is my bag?

| C |

I can't find mine, either...what should we do...the **22.**_____ is getting increasingly fierce...

| A |

break the window to get more **23.**_____...then we go down to the secret **24.**_____

| B |

Fine, I'm taking two adorable **25.**_____ mugs next to the desk **26.**_____ with me...

| C |

Can we go now...I'm having a hard time breathing?

| B |

Perhaps the **27.**_____ from the vase will cause someone ill under normal condition, but when the **28.**_____ is scarce, your body functions better.

| A |

You're saying that you are immune to **29.**_____ monoxide?

| B |

...I'm going to take this **30.**_____ plate as well...

| 參考答案 |

1. control
2. eyesight
3. light
4. dance
5. perception
6. jumping
7. sprinkle
8. quilt
9. pillow
10. sofa
11. ax
12. movie
13. snack
14. fabricating
15. luck
16. corridor
17. extinguisher
18. extinguish
19. migraine
20. pills
21. herbs
22. fire
23. air
24. passage
25. coffee
26. lamp
27. fragrance
28. oxygen
29. carbon
30. elephant

Section 2
Questions 11-20

Write the correct letter, A-J, next to Questions 11-20

A Madame Defarge

B Mr. Edwards

C Lady Bellaston

D Lord Fellamar

E Nightingale

F Mrs Western

G Sophia

H Dr. Manette

I Tom Jones

J Mr. Allworthy

---

11. Previous smart moves come back to bite him
12. the schemer behind getting rid of someone
13. a vivid tale trying to beguile someone
14. conduct a scheme to eliminate the opponent
15. tarnish someone by following the plan
16. receive evidence that can change one's perception
17. in a desperate need of skills for survival
18. make a contribution to overturn one's fate
19. receive evidence that makes one discredit another person's character
20. make accusations through certain commodities

影子跟讀練習 MP3 014

In *A Tale of Two Cities*, we have mentioned about Madame Defarge's revenge by lacing scarfs that contain vile acts of those aristocrats. The wicked Madame Defarge has the document that Dr. Manette wrote during his unfair incarceration. For today's lecture, we will be solely focusing on *The History of Tom Jones, a Founding*, and talk about Lady Bellaston.

在《雙城記》中，我們已經有提過德法奇夫人藉由編織上頭寫有那些貴族罪行的圍巾以進行復仇。邪惡的德法奇夫人持有曼奈特醫生在不公平的冤獄中所撰寫的文件。而今天的講堂，我們只會談論《湯姆‧瓊斯》以及貝拉斯頓夫人。

First, we have to take a look at book 7 chapter 2. Since after the exile from Mr. Allworthy, the central concern for Tom is how to make a living. Let's look at the end of the paragraph. "Every profession, and every trade, required length of time, and what was worse, money; for matters are so constituted, that nothing out of nothing is not a truer maxim in physics than in politics."

首先，我們必須要看下第七卷第二章。既然湯姆被歐渥希逐出家門，對湯姆來說主要的考量是要如何謀生。讓我們看一下最後一個段落。「每一種職業、每一門生意都需要花時間學習或經營，更糟的是還需要投入金錢。因為世事就是如此，無中不能生有不只適用於物理現象，在謀生方面也是如此。」

This further illustrates how hard it is to make a living without professional skills, and to further elucidate, Tom, after living in a wealthy family and having been educated by two great masters, still cannot stand on his own feet.

這進一步闡釋了沒有專業技能要維持生計是有多麼困難的事情，而也進一步地解釋，湯姆儘管出生在富裕的家庭且由兩個老師指導，仍舊無法自力更生。

❶ revenge 復仇
❷ vile 可恥的；邪惡的
❸ aristocrat 貴族（指個人）；具貴族氣派的人
❹ document 文件
❺ maxim 格言，箴言
❻ illustrate 闡釋
❼ professional 專業人士
❽ elucidate 解釋
❾ educate 教育
❿ master 老師

What does this have to do with Lady Bellaston? Then we have to take a look at book 13, chapter 8. A bank note of 50 pounds. It's a generous offer given by Lady Bellaston. So he is now receiving money from the lady to make a living instead of finding a job. With generosity of Lady Bellaston, Tom has become the most decent and glamourous guy in London, and has lived a relatively wealthy life. Tom's love for Sophia prevents him from repaying passions and generosity from Lady Bellaston. According to the statement made from the author, Lady Bellaston is now at the age that is unfavorable for the love to blossom.

這又與貝拉斯頓夫人有什麼關聯呢？那麼，我們就必須要看一下第 13 卷第 8 章。50 磅的銀行票卷。這是貝拉斯頓夫人的慷慨贈與。所以湯姆現在不是靠自己找一份工作維持生計，而是從女人手中拿錢。有著貝拉斯頓夫人的慷慨大方，湯姆已經成了倫敦最得宜且富魅力的男子了，並且過著略為富裕的生活。湯姆對蘇菲亞的愛讓他無法報答貝拉斯頓夫人的激情和慷慨。根據作者所做的陳述，貝拉斯頓夫人處於一個不利於讓愛情開花的時期。

Lady Bellaston soon learns that she has a rival, Sophia, whom Tom falls in love with. Lady Bellaston immediately comes up with a black design by setting Sophia up with a nobleman, who frequently visits her. This nobleman is actually Lord Fellamar. Lord Fellamar is obviously intrigued by Sophia and refers to her as blazing star. He even wants to make a proposal to Sophia.

貝拉斯頓夫人馬上得知了她有個情敵：蘇菲亞，也就是湯姆愛上的女子。貝拉斯頓夫人即刻就想出了陰毒計謀，要將蘇菲亞和一位常拜訪她的高貴人士進行配對。這位高貴人士實際上就是費勒瑪爵爺。費勒瑪爵爺顯然受到蘇菲亞的迷惑，且將其稱為閃耀之星。他甚至想要向蘇菲亞求婚。

Lady Bellaston wants to prove to Lord Fellamar that Sophia is silly in love with Tom Jones. Lady Bellaston uses Mr. Edwards to tell a lie that the corpse of a handsome body is found, which is proclaimed to be the relative of Mr. Allworthy, suggesting that the deceased person is Tom Jones. Sophia is in shock when she learns the news, and faints on the spot. Lord Fellamar is more convincingly than ever that Sophia is in love with Tom, and Lord Fellamar and Lady Bellaston have decided to execute the so called the destructive scheme, but they believe that there is no harm in that since Lord Fellamar really loves Sophia and will marry her right after the scheme. With this plan, Lady Bellaston knows she will soon get rid of her rival, Sophia, and be happily with her lover, Tom.

貝拉斯頓夫人想要向費勒瑪爵爺證明蘇菲亞愚昧地愛上了湯姆瓊斯。貝拉斯頓夫人利用愛德華茲講述一個謊言，就是有一具英俊的男子的屍體，據說是歐渥希的親戚被發現，暗指這個亡者就是湯姆瓊斯。蘇菲亞在聽到這個消息時感到震驚，且當場昏倒了。費勒瑪爵爺比起以往更相信了蘇菲亞愛著湯姆，而費勒瑪爵爺和貝拉斯頓夫人已經決定要一起執行一個毀滅性計畫，但是他們相信這個行動是無傷大雅的，因為費勒瑪爵爺真的愛著蘇菲亞，並且會於計畫結束後與她成親。有了這個計謀，貝拉斯頓夫人知道她能除掉她的情敵蘇菲亞，並與她的愛人湯姆過著快樂的日子。

❶ generous 慷慨的，大方的
❷ receive 收到，接到
❸ generosity 慷慨

❹ glamourous 富魅力的

❺ repay 償還；還錢給

❻ unfavorable 不利的；不適宜的

❼ rival 情敵

❽ a black design 陰毒計謀

❾ proposal 求婚

❿ destructive 毀滅性的

Then with Lord Fellamar's breaking into Sophia's room, the tragic incident marks the beginning. Lord Fellamar begins with the confession of his love, and eventually is followed by his move towards Sophia, which makes her clothes tottered. Although the plan is unsuccessful, Lady Bellaston has done quite a damage to Sophia. Sophia's father has arrived at the scene just in time; otherwise, Sophia will be ravaged by Lord Fellamar.

緊接著，費勒瑪爵爺闖入了蘇菲亞的房間，這悲劇性的事件標誌著事件的開端。費勒瑪爵爺開始了他的愛情告白，而最終伴隨著他朝向蘇菲亞的舉動，讓她的衣服殘破不堪。儘管這個計謀並未成功，貝拉斯頓夫人對蘇菲亞造成了相當程度的傷害。蘇菲亞的父親及時抵達現場，否則，蘇菲亞就要慘遭費勒瑪爵爺的摧殘。

What about Tom? Tom wants to get rid of Lady Bellaston, and under the guidance of his friend, Nightingale, he successfully makes Lady Bellaston enraged by writing letters, pretending that he seriously wants to propose to her.

那湯姆呢？湯姆想要擺脫貝拉斯頓夫人，而在奈丁格爾的指導之下，他成功地使用信件讓貝拉斯頓夫人勃然大怒，假裝自己正經八百的要向她求婚。

Now Tom feels relieved that he won't have to deal with Lady Bellaston. However, what he writes to Lady Bellaston is the living proof that will come back at him later. Lady Bellaston later hands over those letters to Mrs Western, who proclaims that Miss Western will soon be notified. Tom eventually gets a letter from Sophia, stating that she has the proof of Tom's proposal to Lady Bellaston, and during which Tom writes a letter to Sophia that he is worried about her, suggesting that Tom was pursuing two people at the same time. Lady Bellaston's destructive plan to Tom also works exceedingly well, making Sophia doubtful about Tom's character as a person...I guess that's the end of the today's class...

現在湯姆感到如釋重負，他不必再應付貝拉斯頓夫人了。然而，他所寫給貝拉斯頓夫人的信就是活生生的證據，且會在之後反咬自己。貝拉斯頓夫人稍後將這封信遞交給威斯頓女士，她宣稱威斯頓小姐會立即知曉。湯姆最終收到了蘇菲亞的信件，上面寫著，她有湯姆向貝拉斯頓夫人求婚的證據，而在這段期間，湯姆也同樣寫信給蘇菲亞說，自己很擔心她，暗示著湯姆在同個時間點追求兩位女子。貝拉斯頓夫人對湯姆的毀滅性計畫也進行得異常圓滿，讓蘇菲亞對湯姆的人格有所懷疑……我想今天的課堂就到此結束了…

（註：威斯頓小姐指的就是蘇菲亞。）

❶ tragic 悲劇性的

❷ confession 坦白，供認

❸ totter 蹣跚，踉蹌

❹ unsuccessful 不成功的；失敗的

❺ damage 損害；損失

❻ ravage 毀滅，毀壞

❼ enrage 激怒；使憤怒

❽ relieved 如釋重負

❾ proclaim 宣告；公布

❿ proof 證據

試題解析

- 第 **11** 題，Previous smart moves come back to bite him，對應到 Tom eventually gets a letter from Sophia, stating that she has the proof of Tom's proposal to Lady Bellaston, and during which Tom writes a letter to Sophia that he is worried about her, suggesting that Tom was pursuing two people at the same time，湯姆自以為的智計，反倒成了鐵證，就是他周遊在兩個女子之間，這也讓他對蘇菲亞的求愛失敗，蘇菲亞因此而不信他，故答案要選 **I** Tom Jones。

- 第 **12** 題，the schemer behind getting rid of someone，對應到 Tom wants to get rid of Lady Bellaston, and under the guidance of his friend, Nightingale, he successfully makes Lady Bellaston enraged by writing letters, pretending that he seriously wants to propose to her. Now Tom feels relieved that he won't have to deal with Lady Bellaston，是 Nightingale 獻計，所以他是幕後策畫的人，故答案要選 **E** Nightingale。

- 第 **13** 題，a vivid tale trying to beguile someone，對應到 Lady Bellaston uses Mr. Edwards to tell a lie that the corpse of a handsome body is found, which is proclaimed to be the relative of Mr. Allworthy, suggesting that the deceased person is Tom Jones，a vivid tale trying to beguile = Mr. Edwards to tell a lie，故答案要選 **B** Mr. Edwards。

- 第 14 題，conduct a scheme to eliminate the opponent，對應到 With this plan, Lady Bellaston knows she will soon get rid of her rival, Sophia, and be happily with her lover, Tom，eliminate the opponent = get rid of her rival，故答案要選 **C** Lady Bellaston。

- 第 15 題，tarnish someone by following the plan，對應到 Lord Fellamar begins with the confession of his love, and eventually is followed by his move towards Sophia, which makes her clothes tottered，tarnish = makes her clothes tottered，指玷汙了蘇菲亞，故答案要選 **D** Lord Fellamar。

- 第 16 題，receive evidence that can change one's perception，對應到 Lady Bellaston later hands over those letters to Mrs Western, who proclaims that Miss Western will soon be notified，是威斯頓女士收到證據，而這個證據能改變一個人的看法，指的就是這個證據能夠改變蘇菲亞對湯姆的印象，故答案要選 **F** Mrs Western。

- 第 17 題，in a desperate need of skills for survival，對應到 Since after the exile from Mr. Allworthy, the central concern for Tom is how to make a living，the central concern for Tom is how to make a living = in a desperate need of skills for survival，故答案要選 **I** Tom Jones。

- **第 18 題**，make a contribution to overturn one's fate，對應到 So he is now receiving money from the lady to make a living instead of finding a job. With generosity of Lady Bellaston, Tom has become the most decent and glamourous guy in London, and has lived a relatively wealthy life，contribution = receiving money，overturn one's fate = has lived a relatively wealthy life，因為這些金錢翻轉了湯姆的命運，故答案要選 **C** Lady Bellaston。

- **第 19 題**，receive evidence that makes one discredit another person's character，對應到 Tom eventually gets a letter from Sophia, stating that she has the proof of Tom's proposal to Lady Bellaston, and during which Tom writes a letter to Sophia that he is worried about her, suggesting that Tom was pursuing two people at the same time，收到證據，而不採信另一個人的說詞或不信任對方的人格，指的就是蘇菲亞，故答案要選 **G** Sophia。

- **第 20 題**，make accusations through certain commodities，對應到 In *A Tale of Two Cities*, we have mentioned about Madame Defarge's revenge by lacing scarfs that contain vile acts of those aristocrats，commodities = scarfs，vile acts of those aristocrats = make accusations，指的就是透過這些進行其惡行的指控，故答案要選 **A** Madame Defarge。

▶▶ 填空測驗

| Instruction | MP3 001

現在請再聽一次音檔，並做下列的測驗，檢視自己能否完成此填空測驗和強化自己聽力能力和拼字能力，降低並修正自己漏聽到聽力訊息的機會，大幅提升應考實力。

In *A Tale of Two Cities*, we have mentioned about Madame Defarge's revenge by lacing **1.**_____ that contain vile acts of those aristocrats. The wicked Madame Defarge has the document that Dr. Manette wrote during his unfair incarceration. For today's lecture, we will be solely focusing on *The History of Tom Jones, a Founding*, and talk about Lady Bellaston.

First, we have to take a look at book 7 chapter **2.** Since after the exile from Mr. Allworthy, the central concern for Tom is how to make a living. Let's look at the end of the paragraph. "Every profession, and every trade, required length of time, and what was worse, money; for matters are so constituted, that nothing out of nothing is not a truer maxim in **2.**_____ than in politics."

This further illustrates how hard it is to make a living without professional skills, and to further **3.**_____, Tom, after living in a wealthy family and having been educated by two great masters, still cannot stand on his own **4.**_____.

What does this have to do with Lady Bellaston? Then we have to take a look at book 13, chapter **8.** A bank note of 50 pounds. It's a generous offer given by Lady Bellaston. So he is now receiving money from the lady to make a living instead of finding a job. With generosity of Lady Bellaston, Tom has become the most decent and **5.**_____ guy in London, and has lived a relatively wealthy life. Tom's love for Sophia prevents him from **6.**_____ passions and generosity from Lady Bellaston. According to the statement made from the author, Lady Bellaston is now at the age that is **7.**_____ for the love to blossom.

Lady Bellaston soon learns that she has a **8.**_____, Sophia, whom Tom falls in love with. Lady Bellaston immediately comes up with a **9.**_____ design by setting Sophia up with a nobleman, who frequently visits her. This nobleman is actually Lord Fellamar. Lord Fellamar is obviously **10.**_____ by Sophia and refers to her as blazing **11.**_____. He even wants to make a proposal to Sophia.

Lady Bellaston wants to prove to Lord Fellamar that Sophia is silly in love with Tom Jones. Lady Bellaston uses Mr. Edwards to tell a lie that the **12.**_____ of a **13.**_____ body is found, which is proclaimed to be the relative of Mr. Allworthy, suggesting that the **14.**_____ person is Tom Jones. Sophia is in shock when she learns the news, and faints on the spot. Lord Fellamar is more **15.**_____ than ever that Sophia is in love with Tom, and Lord Fellamar and Lady Bellaston have decided to **16.**_____ the so called the destructive scheme, but they believe that there is no **17.**_____ in that since Lord Fellamar really loves Sophia and will marry her right after the scheme. With this plan, Lady Bellaston knows she will soon get rid of her rival, Sophia, and be **18.**_____ with her lover, Tom.

Then with Lord Fellamar's breaking into Sophia's room, the **19.**__ _____ incident marks the beginning. Lord Fellamar begins with the **20.**_____ of his love, and eventually is followed by his move towards Sophia, which makes her **21.**_____ tottered. Although the plan is unsuccessful, Lady Bellaston has done quite a **22.**_____ to Sophia. Sophia's father has arrived at the scene just in time; otherwise, Sophia will be **23.**_____ by Lord Fellamar.

What about Tom? Tom wants to get rid of Lady Bellaston, and under the **24.**_____ of his friend, Nightingale, he successfully makes Lady Bellaston enraged by writing letters, pretending that he seriously wants to **25.**_____ to her. Now Tom feels relieved that he won't have to deal with Lady Bellaston. However, what he writes to Lady Bellaston is the living **26.**_____ that will come back at him later. Lady Bellaston later hands over those letters to Mrs Western, who proclaims that Miss Western will soon be **27.**_____. Tom eventually gets a letter from Sophia, stating that she has the proof of Tom's **28.**_____ to Lady Bellaston, and during which Tom writes a letter to Sophia that he is worried about her, suggesting that Tom was pursuing two people at the same time. Lady Bellaston's **29.**_____ plan to Tom also works exceedingly well, making Sophia **30.**_____ about Tom's character as a person...I guess that's the end of the today's class...

參考答案

1. scarfs
2. physics
3. elucidate
4. feet
5. glamourous
6. repaying
7. unfavorable
8. rival
9. black
10. intrigued
11. star
12. corpse
13. handsome
14. deceased
15. convincingly
16. execute
17. harm
18. happily
19. tragic
20. confession
21. clothes
22. damage
23. ravaged
24. guidance
25. propose
26. proof
27. notified
28. proposal
29. destructive
30. doubtful

Section 3 Questions 21-30

21. almost becoming one's victim
22. one's smugness has greatly affected one's judgment
23. one's resentfulness towards someone has become greater because of the refusal
24. one's inability of discerning another's customs
25. one's postponement is due to others' influence
26. one's hiding of certain truth has caused another to suffer
27. one's fortune is the drive for the crime
28. one's sincerity has been helpful for one's discernment
29. one's slander has caused another's distaste for someone
30. one's emotions are greatly affected after the conversation

Questions 21-30

Write the correct letter, A-G, next to Questions 21-30

You may use some of the letters more than once

A Bingley

B Elizabeth

C Mr. Darcy

D Elizabeth's sister

E Mr. Wickham

F Mr. Darcy's sister

G late Mr. Darcy

影子跟讀練習 MP3 015

做完題目後，除了對答案知道錯的部分在哪外，更重要的是要修正自己聽力根本的問題，即聽力理解力和聽力專注力，聽力專注力的修正能逐步強化本身的聽力實力，所以現在請根據聽力內容「逐個段落」、「數個段落」或「整篇」進行跟讀練習，提升在實際考場時專注聽完每個訊息、定位出關鍵考點和搭配筆記回答完所有題目。Go!

At the ball, "tolerable", a comment about Elizabeth's appearance by Mr. Darcy has resulted a terrible misunderstanding between him and Elizabeth. Elizabeth's aversion to Mr. Darcy has been aggravated by Mr. Wickham's conversations with her, her understanding about Mr. Darcy, and what others think of Mr. Darcy.

在舞會上，達西先生對伊麗莎白外表「還能看」的評論導致了他和伊麗莎白之間的誤會。伊麗莎白對達西先生的嫌惡也因為她與威克漢姆的對話、伊麗莎白對達西先生的了解和其他人對達西先生評價而惡化。

We have to flip to chapter 24 because we have to finish this fiction in two weeks. "The whole of what Elizabeth had already heard, his claims on Mr. Darcy, and all that he had suffered from him, was now openly acknowledged and publicly canvassed." Elizabeth cannot help but have the feeling that her opinion about Mr. Darcy is right all along, and her sister seems to have a different opinion that they might be mistaken about Mr. Darcy. Her kindness serves as a great tool in not judging someone unfairly.

我們必須要跳到第 24 章，因為我們在兩週內要結束這本小說。「自己曾吃了他多大的虧，伊麗莎白此前已經聽說了，如今更是人盡皆知，還公開被拿出來議論。」伊麗莎白不得不有那種感覺，就是她對達西先生的看法由始至終都對極了，而她的姐姐似乎有不同的看法，認為他們可能誤解達西先生了。她的善良充當了很好的解方，而不會不公正地評價一個人。

❶ tolerable 可忍受的；可容忍的

❷ comment 意見，評論

❸ conversation 會話，談話

❹ acknowledge 承認

❺ publicly 公開地，公然地

❻ canvass 仔細審議；詳細討論

❼ kindness 仁慈；和藹；好意

❽ unfairly 不公平地；不公正地

In chapter 34, Mr. Darcy's boldness in confessing his love to Elizabeth has marked a great beginning for the two. Elizabeth's inability to be grateful of Mr. Darcy's love and her interpretation of his love as "somewhat reluctant", have made Mr. Darcy question about Elizabeth's rebuff. This has served a great way for the two to get to know what's on each other's mind. Elizabeth's feelings towards Mr. Darcy are mixed with the anger that he destroys her sister's happiness with Bingley and his atrocious act towards Mr. Wickham. To which, Mr. Darcy does not gainsay anything, and the following conversation goes unpleasant for the two, making Elizabeth distraught.

在第 34 章，達西先生勇敢向伊麗莎白示愛標誌著兩人之間很棒的開

端。對於達西先生的示愛，伊麗莎白無法為此而心懷感恩，她將達西先生的愛詮釋成「這有些勉強」，也讓達西先生質疑伊麗莎白的斷然拒絕。這也充當了很好的方式，讓兩個人能夠了解彼此心裡都在想些什麼。伊麗莎白對達西先生的感覺摻雜了憤怒，因為達西毀掉了自己的姐姐與賓利的快樂幸福，還有達西對威克漢姆的殘暴行徑。對此達西並不想否認什麼，而接續的對話讓彼此都感到不愉快，這也讓伊麗莎白心煩意亂。

Luckily, in next chapter, a long letter from Mr. Darcy will clear up all the misunderstandings. Mr. Darcy notices Bingley is captivated by his sister, and while her sister is accepting all the gestures and love from Bingley, she doesn't seem to fall in love with him deeply. The disparity between two family seems to be the greatest hindrance for their love to blossom. His pointing out to Bingley does make Bingley hesitate over, and his resolution eventually wavers; therefore, procrastinating his plan. He further confesses his concealment about Elizabeth's sister is in town, the only reason that does not make Mr. Darcy's mind peaceful. All in all, he thinks this is his innocent mistake, and will not make a further attempt to say sorry.

幸運的是，在下一個章節，達西先生的一封長信就能讓所有誤會都釐清了。達西先生注意到賓利受到她姐姐的吸引，而當她姐姐接受了賓利的所有好意和愛意時，她姐姐似乎並未深愛著賓利。兩家人的差距也似乎是讓他們兩人的愛開花結果的最大阻饒。他向賓利的剖析也讓賓利猶豫著，最終賓利的決心動搖了，也因此延宕的他的計畫。達西進一步地坦承他對於隱瞞伊麗莎白的姐姐在城內，是唯一一個讓達西先生心無法平靜的原因。從各方面來說，達西認為這是他的無心之失，而不會再為此而道歉。

❶ boldness 勇敢；大膽

❷ inability 無能；無力

❸ reluctant 不情願的；勉強的

❹ atrocious 兇暴的；殘酷的

❺ gainsay 否認；反駁

❻ unpleasant 使人不愉快的；不中意的

❼ distraught 心煩意亂的

❽ captivate 使著迷；蠱惑

❾ blossom 開花；生長茂盛

❿ procrastinate 延遲；耽擱

As for Mr. Wickham, Mr. Darcy's father thinks highly of him, enjoys socializing with him, and offers the opportunity to him. Mr. Wickham has several bad habits, but the late Mr. Darcy is not able to witness. Mr. Wickham eventually gets the inheritance from the late Mr. Darcy, a thousand pounds, and then as a compensation for not being a clergyman, Mr. Darcy gives him three thousand pounds. Then Mr. Wickham lives an idle life. Three years later, Mr. Wickham begs Mr. Darcy to grant him the position of the clergyman, saying that studying law does not seem to be profitable. However, Mr. Darcy declines his offer repeatedly, and Mr. Wickham's situation goes from bad to worse, making his rancor towards Mr. Darcy increasingly greater.

而關於威克漢姆，達西先生的父親看重他，也享受與威克漢姆來往，並且提供了機會給他。威克漢姆有幾項壞習慣，但老達西先生無法親眼目睹。威克漢姆最終得到的老達西的遺產一千磅，而接著要補償威克漢姆不能當牧師，達西又給了威克漢姆三千磅。然後，威克漢姆就這樣閒賦無事。三年後，威克漢姆向達西先生乞求他批准牧師職位，説道研讀法律似乎不是有利可圖的。然而，達西先生一再地拒絕他的請求，而威克漢姆的情況日益走下坡，讓他對達西先生的怨恨也與日俱增。

Another thing awful about Mr. Wickham is his agenda on Mr. Darcy's sister, who is only 15. He sets his sights on her inheritance, which is three thousand pounds. Fortunately, Mr. Wickham's agenda was unsuccessful.

威克漢姆另一個糟糕的地方是他對達西先生年僅 15 歲的妹妹的計謀。他將目標鎖定在她三千磅的遺產上。幸運的是，威克漢姆的計畫並未奏效。

After repeated reading the letter over and over, it soon makes Mr. Darcy's conduct blameless. How can a guy like Mr. Wickham paint a vivid picture about how things actually happen, beguiling people around them? How can a person like Mr. Darcy to be easily misunderstood, getting prejudiced by others. But Elizabeth clearly has a bias against Mr. Darcy after his comment about her as someone tolerable. We cannot deny the fact that Elizabeth is the one who cannot think clearly. Mr. Wickham's actions are contradictory in many ways, but Elizabeth chooses not to discern.

在反覆閱讀信件後，馬上讓達西先生的行為無可指責。一個像威克漢姆這樣的男子怎麼能夠栩栩如生地描繪出一個實際上確實發生的事，蒙騙他周遭的所有人呢？而像達西先生這樣的人又怎麼會容易受人誤解且讓其他人對他有偏見？但是，伊麗莎白很明確地在達西先生對她外表評論成還能看的時候就對他有偏見了。我們不能否認一點，就是伊麗莎白才是無法清楚思考的人。威克漢姆的行為在許多面向上都有矛盾之處，但是伊麗莎白卻選擇不去分辨。

I think the author is making a great point here by pointing out something. We tend to feel offended by others who have shown the slightest interest in us, and we are pleased by those who do the superficial stuff well, saying what "we would like to here; therefore, locking doors for those who seem aloof to us. Vanity is an evil trait that makes invisible to facts presenting in front of our eyes. Elizabeth's clairvoyance in men has been greatly slashed by her vanity. That is quite a contrary to her sister, who has demonstrated her integrity and generosity...

我想作者在這裡，藉由點出某件事來提出一個重要主張。那些對我們顯示出有點興趣缺缺的人，讓我們傾向覺得自己受到了冒犯，而卻對於那些表面功夫做得很好的人感到滿意，說道我們因而對那些對我們似乎冷漠的人關起了大門。虛榮心這個邪惡的特質，讓許多在我們眼前所呈現出的事實都隱形不可見。伊麗莎白對男人的洞察力也因為自己本身的虛榮心而受到大幅削弱了。這與她姐姐所展現出的正直和慷慨特質是相當大相逕庭的...。

❶ opportunity 機會

❷ inheritance 繼承物；遺產

❸ profitable 有利潤的、有利益的

❹ repeatedly 重複地

❺ agenda 待議諸事項；議程

❻ blameless 無可責備的；無過失的

❼ beguile 欺騙，詭騙

❽ contradictory 矛盾的，對立的

❾ discern 分辨，識別

❿ superficial 膚淺的，淺薄的

試題解析

● 第 **21** 題，almost becoming one's victim，對應到 Fortunately, Mr. Wickham's agenda was unsuccessful，也因為 Mr. Wickham 計謀沒有成功，但這個計謀幾乎要讓達西先生的妹妹成為犧牲者，故答案要選 **F** Mr. Darcy's sister。

● 第 **22** 題，one's **smugness** has greatly affected one's judgment，對應到 Elizabeth's clairvoyance in men has greatly been slashed by her vanity. That is quite a contrary to her sister, who has demonstrated her integrity and generosity...，就是過度自滿自己的判斷力，才會造成判斷錯誤，故答案要選 **B** Elizabeth。

● 第 **23** 題，one's **resentfulness** towards someone has become greater because of the refusal，對應到 However, Mr. Darcy declines his offer repeatedly, and Mr. Wickham's situation goes from bad to worse, making his rancor towards Mr. Darcy increasingly greater，**resentfulness** = rancor，故答案要選 **E** Mr. Wickham。

● 第 **24** 題，one's **inability** of discerning another's customs，對應到 Mr. Wickham has several bad habits, but the late Mr. Darcy is not able to witness，**inability** = not able to witness，故答案要選 **G** late Mr. Darcy。

- **第 25 題**，one's **postponement** is due to others' influence，對應到 His pointing out to Bingley does make Bingley hesitate over, and his resolution eventually wavers; therefore, procrastinating his plan，**postponement** = procrastinating，故答案要選 **A** Bingley。

- **第 26 題**，one's **hiding** of certain truth has caused another to suffer，對應到 He further confesses his concealment about Elizabeth's sister is in town, the only reason that does not make Mr. Darcy's mind peaceful，**hiding** = concealment，故答案要選 **C** Mr. Darcy。

- **第 27 題**，one's **fortune** is the drive for the crime，對應到 Another thing awful about Mr. Wickham is his agenda on Mr. Darcy's sister, who is only 15. He sets his sights on her inheritance, which is three thousand pounds，**fortune** = inheritance，故答案要選 **F** Mr. Darcy's sister。

- **第 28 題**，one's **sincerity** has been helpful for one's discernment，對應到 Her kindness serves as a great tool in not judging someone unfairly 和 That is quite a contrary to her sister, who has demonstrated her integrity and generosity...，**sincerity** = kindness，故答案要選 **D** Elizabeth's sister。

● **第 29 題**，one's **slander** has caused another's distaste for someone，對應到 "The whole of what Elizabeth had already heard, his claims on Mr. Darcy, and all that he had suffered from him, was now openly acknowledged and publicly canvassed." Elizabeth cannot help but have the feeling that her opinion about Mr. Darcy is right all along，**slander** = his claims on Mr. Darcy，another's distaste for someone = her opinion about Mr. Darcy is right all along，故答案要選 **E** Mr. Wickham。

● **第 30 題**，one's **emotions** are greatly affected after the conversation，對應到 Mr. Darcy does not gainsay anything, and the following conversation goes unpleasant for the two, making Elizabeth distraught，關鍵字是 distraught，Elizabeth 在對話後感到心煩意亂，等同於 **emotions** are greatly affected，故答案要選 **B** Elizabeth。

▶▶ 填空測驗

　　現在請再聽一次音檔，並做下列的測驗，檢視自己能否完成此填空測驗和強化自己聽力能力和拼字能力，降低並修正自己漏聽到聽力訊息的機會，大幅提升應考實力。

　　At the ball, "tolerable", a comment about Elizabeth's **1.**_____ by Mr. Darcy has resulted a terrible misunderstanding between him and Elizabeth. Elizabeth's **2.**_____ to Mr. Darcy has been aggravated by Mr. Wickham's conversations with her, her understanding about Mr. Darcy, and what others think of Mr. Darcy.

　　We have to flip to chapter 24 because we have to finish this fiction in two weeks. "The whole of what Elizabeth had already heard, his claims on Mr. Darcy, and all that he had suffered from him, was now openly **3.**_____ and publicly **4.**_____." Elizabeth cannot help but have the feeling that her opinion about Mr. Darcy is right all along, and her sister seems to have a different opinion that they might be mistaken about Mr. Darcy. Her **5.**_____ serves as a great tool in not judging someone unfairly.

　　In chapter 34, Mr. Darcy's boldness in confessing his love to Elizabeth has marked a great beginning for the two. Elizabeth's inability to be grateful of Mr. Darcy's love and her interpretation of his love as "somewhat **6.**_____", have made Mr. Darcy question about Elizabeth's **7.**_____. This has served a great way for the two to get to know what's on each other's mind. Elizabeth's feelings towards Mr. Darcy are mixed with the anger that he destroys her sister's happiness with Bingley and his **8.**_____ act towards Mr. Wickham. To which, Mr. Darcy does not gainsay anything, and the following conversation goes unpleasant for the two, making Elizabeth **9.**_____.

Luckily, in next chapter, a long letter from Mr. Darcy will clear up all the misunderstandings. Mr. Darcy notices Bingley is **10.**_____ by his sister, and while her sister is accepting all the gestures and love from Bingley, she doesn't seem to fall in love with him deeply. The **10.**_____disparity between two family seems to be the greatest **11.**_____ for their love to blossom. His pointing out to Bingley does make Bingley hesitate over, and his resolution eventually wavers; therefore, procrastinating his plan. He further confesses his **12.**_____ about Elizabeth's sister is in town, the only reason that does not make Mr. Darcy's mind peaceful. All in all, he thinks this is his **13.**_____ mistake, and will not make a further attempt to say sorry.

As for Mr. Wickham, Mr. Darcy's father thinks highly of him, enjoys socializing with him, and offers the **14.**_____ to him. Mr. Wickham has several bad habits, but the late Mr. Darcy is not able to witness. Mr. Wickham eventually gets the inheritance from the late Mr. Darcy, a thousand pounds, and then as a **15.**_____ for not being a clergyman, Mr. Darcy gives him three thousand pounds. Then Mr. Wickham lives an idle life. Three years later, Mr. Wickham begs

Mr. Darcy to grant him the position of the clergyman, saying that studying law does not seem to be **16.**_____. However, Mr. Darcy declines his offer repeatedly, and Mr. Wickham's situation goes from bad to worse, making his **17.**_____ towards Mr. Darcy increasingly greater.

Another thing awful about Mr. Wickham is his agenda on Mr. Darcy's sister, who is only **15.** He sets his sights on her **18.**_____, which is three thousand pounds. Fortunately, Mr. Wickham's agenda was **19.**_____.

After repeated reading the letter over and over, it soon makes Mr. Darcy's **20.**_____ blameless. How can a guy like Mr. Wickham paint a vivid picture about how things actually happen, beguiling people around them? How can a person like Mr. Darcy to be easily misunderstood, getting **21.**_____ by others. But Elizabeth clearly has a bias against Mr. Darcy after his comment about her as someone **22.**_____. We cannot deny the fact that Elizabeth is the one who cannot think clearly. Mr. Wickham's actions are contradictory in many ways, but Elizabeth chooses not to **23.**_____.

I think the author is making a great point here by pointing out something. We tend to feel **24.**_____ by others who have shown the slightest interest in us, and we are pleased by those who do the **25.**_____ stuff well, saying what "we would like to here; therefore, locking doors for those who seem **26.**_____ to us.

Vanity is an evil trait that makes **27.**＿＿＿＿＿＿ to facts presenting in front of our eyes. Elizabeth's **28.**＿＿＿＿＿＿ in men has been greatly slashed by her **29.**＿＿＿＿＿. That is quite a contrary to her sister, who has demonstrated her **30.**＿＿＿＿＿＿ and generosity...

| 參考答案 |

1.	appearance	2.	aversion
3.	acknowledged	4.	canvassed
5.	kindness	6.	reluctant
7.	rebuff	8.	atrocious
9.	distraught	10.	captivated
11.	hindrance	12.	concealment
13.	innocent	14.	opportunity
15.	compensation	16.	profitable
17.	rancor	18.	inheritance
19.	unsuccessful	20.	conduct
21.	prejudiced	22.	tolerable
23.	discern	24.	offended
25.	superficial	26.	aloof
27.	invisible	28.	clairvoyance
29.	vanity	30.	integrity

Section 4 Questions 31-32
Complete the Notes below
Write No More Than Two Words for each answer

In *Walden*, the red squirrel, roaming freely on the rooftop and running in such a haste would arrive at the field, trying to find suitable **31.**_____.

In *The Forest Unseen*, the gray squirrel would not **32.**_____ ____ on the leaf litter. Instead, it bumps its nose into the leaf litter.

Questions 33-40
Complete the diagram below
Write No More Than Two Words for each answer
Write your answers in boxes 33-40 on your answer sheet

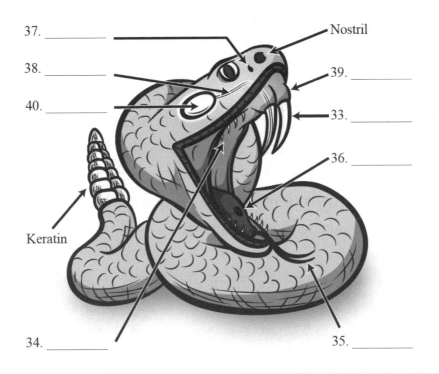

37. _____   Nostril

38. _____

39. _____

40. _____

33. _____

36. _____

Keratin

34. _____   35. _____

---

glottis: the part of the larynx consisting of the vocal cords and the opening between them.

pit: a large hole in the ground, or a slightly low area in any surface

sheath: a structure in living tissue which closely envelops another

duct: a tube or pipe that carries liquid or air, especially in and out of buildings or through the body

做完題目後，除了對答案知道錯的部分在哪外，更重要的是要修正自己聽力根本的問題，即聽力理解力和聽力專注力，聽力專注力的修正能逐步強化本身的聽力實力，所以現在請根據聽力內容「逐個段落」、「數個段落」或「整篇」進行跟讀練習，提升在實際考場時專注聽完每個訊息、定位出關鍵考點和搭配筆記回答完所有題目。Go!

What seems to be a casual, agreeable afternoon in the forest can still contain many hazards concealed. In the forest, for an insect, maintaining a life for a few minutes can be considered a great achievement. What about in the case of squirrels? This is what we will be talking about during today's lecture.

在森林裡，看似愜意、宜人的午後仍可能有著許多危險藏匿其中。在森林裡，對一隻昆蟲來說，維持幾分鐘的存活就能視為是項偉大的成就了。對於松鼠來説又會是如何？這就是我們今天課堂中會談論到的。

In *Walden*, the author mentions the red squirrel, and it certainly is in the paradise, roaming freely on the rooftop and running in such a haste. The red squirrel would arrive at the field, reaching the corn to get the fitting ear. Sometimes with another new ear, and randomly toss away not yet finished cobs. Then he would choose another corn, larger than himself, taking it back to the place where he lives. What a casual life? The depiction of the red squirrel certainly only gives us one of the glimpse lives in the forest. A day like this is like a dream. Most of the time, most animals whether they are predators or preys do need to find the food, shelters, and most important of all, evade predators or confront with the predator.

在《瓦爾登湖》中，作者提到了紅松鼠，而牠在那就像置身在天堂中，自由地漫步在屋頂上，並以如此快速的速度奔跑。紅松鼠會抵達田野，觸及玉米以選取合適的玉米穗。有時候會取另一個新的玉米穗，然後又隨意地丟棄尚未吃完的玉米穗軸。然後，松鼠會選擇比自己體型更大的玉米，將其帶回到自己居住的地方。多麼愜意的生活啊！這樣對紅松鼠的描述僅能讓我們瞥見森林的其中一部份。像這樣度過一天就像一場夢一樣。大多數的時候，大多數的動物，不論其是掠食者或是被捕食者，都會需要找尋食物、庇護所，以及最重要的是，躲避掠食者或正面迎戰掠食者。

So what about the life of the squirrel described by another author in *The Forest Unseen*. The depiction of the gray squirrel in a clumsy way. Instead of swaggering on the leaf litter, it bumps its nose into the leaf litter.

那麼關於在另一本書《森林的秘境》中，所描述的松鼠的生活又是如何？本書描述了灰色松鼠以笨拙的方式生活。灰色松鼠的鼻子撞進葉子裡，而非在葉子上頭昂首闊步。

❶ agreeable 宜人的
❷ hazard 危險
❸ paradise 天堂
❹ cob 玉米穗軸
❺ ear 玉米穗
❻ depiction 描述

❼ glimpse 瞥見；一瞥

❽ predator 掠食者

❾ prey 被捕食者

❿ confront 撞見；勇敢地面對

By discussing these two books briefly, we are not yet mentioning something real and something danger. And we are about to... the danger is actually everywhere? What about those scenes that we frequently see in nature documentaries? An owl chasing down the squirrel, and with its claws grasping the squirrel alive. Or the feisty squirrel mom, which demonstrates its bravery by confronting directly with the rattlesnake?

藉由討論這兩本書籍，我們都尚未提到一些真實且危險的部分。而...我們也正要談論這部份了...實際上，任何地方都危險...那些我們在自然紀錄片中所頻繁看見的場景？一隻貓頭鷹追逐著松鼠，而隨著貓頭鷹爪子攫住活著的松鼠。又或是爭強好勝的松鼠媽媽，展示其勇氣而直接與響尾蛇正面衝突？

Or the cocky squirrel, which obviously bites off more than he can chew, and gets eaten by the cobra? Or the smart squirrel, which makes itself appear larger than normal so that the snake is dissuaded and then retreats. Or a group of squirrels circling around a few baby squirrels? Or a real fight-to-the-death scene between the squirrel and the king cobra. These are all authentic scenes that actually occur every moment.

或是自大的松鼠，顯然是不自量力，而最後被眼鏡蛇吃掉了？或是聰明的松鼠，讓自己的體態顯得比平常更為大隻，這樣一來蛇就會被勸阻，然後撤退了。或是一群松鼠圍繞著幾個幼兒松鼠？或是一個松鼠與眼鏡蛇之間的真實生死鬥場景。這些都是每個時刻當下實際上所發生的真實場景。

The swiftness of the squirrels certainly makes them not that easily to be eaten and remain unharmed under a few strikes of the king cobra. However, the king cobra does have something that is frightening, especially when they are larger. King cobras do possess a fatal neurotoxic venom that can do a great deal of damage to the prey. So let's move on to the anatomy of the rattlesnake.

松鼠的迅捷確實可以讓牠們更不易受到捕食且在眼鏡蛇的幾次攻擊下維持毫髮無傷。然而，眼鏡蛇也有些令人畏懼的部分，特別是當牠們的體型看起來更大隻。眼鏡蛇確實有著致命的神經毒素能對獵物造成很大的傷害。所以讓我們將主題移至響尾蛇的解剖構造上。

❶ nature documentaries 自然紀錄片
❷ bravery 勇敢，勇氣 [U]
❸ rattlesnake 響尾蛇
❹ cocky 自大的
❺ cobra 眼鏡蛇
❻ authentic 可信的，真實的
❼ swiftness 迅捷
❽ unharmed 毫髮無傷
❾ dissuade 勸阻
❿ neurotoxic 毒害神經的

Rattlesnakes are known for their rattles at the end of the tails. Vibrations of the rattle will generate a loud noise that can be served as a warning to others. King snakes; however, are not afraid of this trick.

響尾蛇以牠們尾部的響環而聞名。響環的震動會產生很大的聲音,且能充當成對其他人的警告。然而,王蛇卻不怕這種詭計。

Let's take a look at the anatomy of the rattlesnakes. Their heads are comprised of many important parts that make them fearsome. There are two hollow, retractable **fangs** that can be clearly seen in the graph. Through these fangs, powerful venom can be injected into the prey's body. Beneath these two large fangs, there are **small teeth** in a row to assist their consumption of the prey. When you look at the part near the jaw, there is a **forked tongue** that lies between these teeth.

讓我們看一下響尾蛇的解剖構造。響尾蛇的頭部有許多重要部分,所以讓他們看起來令人生畏。有兩個中空、可縮回的毒牙,可以在圖表中清楚看見。透過這些毒牙,強而有力的毒液可以注射到獵物的身體上。在這兩個毒牙之下,有小的牙齒,這些牙齒成一排以協助牠們攝食獵物。當你看到接近顎的部分,有分岔的舌頭位於這些牙齒中間。

The tongue can serve as a great tool to sense the prey nearby. And there is an expendable **glottis** that is behind the tongue. The function of the glottis is to help them make an air exchange while ingesting prey.

舌頭能充當很好的工具去感知鄰近的獵物。而可消耗的聲門在舌頭後方。聲門的功用是協助牠們在攝食獵物時能進行氣體交換。

Let's take a look at the nostril of the rattlesnake. The nostril and the tongue all assist the rattlesnake to sense olfactory stimuli. Near the nose, there is a heat sensing **pit**. Both the heat sensing pit and the eyes of the rattlesnake are able to sense radiation so that they get to find the prey and make a movement. Beneath it, there is a **venom duct** that transports the venom to larger fangs. The outer cover is the **fang sheath**. What about the **venom gland**? It's an oval shape. Finally, we have to talk about the rattle. It is made up of hollow segments. Keratin makes these segments. The noise that we hear is caused by the vibrations of these segments...

讓我們看下響尾蛇的鼻子。鼻子和舌頭都協助響尾蛇感受嗅覺的的刺激。在靠近鼻子處，有個熱感應窩孔。熱感知的坑和響尾蛇的眼睛能夠感應發熱，這樣一來牠們可以找到獵物並進行移動。在這下方，有個毒液的輸送管，用於將毒液運送到較大的毒牙上。在最外的覆蓋物則是毒牙的護套。那毒液腺體呢？其則是橄欖狀。最後，我們必須要談論下響環。響環是由中空的節所組成的。角質製造這些節。我們所聽到的聲響是由這些節的震動所引起的...。

註：heat-sensing pit 指熱感應窩孔，其位於窩頰上，內有窩頰器官，用於感應紅外線。

❶ rattle 響環
❷ vibration 震動

273

❸ retractable 可縮回的

❹ fangs 毒牙

❺ forked 分岔的

❻ expendable 可消耗的

❼ glottis 聲門

❽ ingest 攝食

❾ pit 窪坑，凹處；地窖等意思，此指蛇的窩孔

❿ venom duct 毒液輸送管

試題解析

- 第 **31** 題，In *Walden*, the red squirrel, roaming freely on the rooftop and running in such a haste would arrive at the field, trying to find suitable **31._____**，故答案為 **ear**。

- 第 **32** 題，In *The Forest Unseen*, the gray squirrel would not **32._____** on the leaf litter. Instead, it bumps its nose into the leaf litter，故答案為 **swagger**。

- 第 **33** 題，觀看圖表並對應到 Their heads are comprised of many important parts that make them fearsome. There are two hollow, retractable **fangs** that can be clearly seen in the graph，故答案為 **fangs**。

- 第 **34** 題，觀看圖表並對應到 Through these fangs, powerful venom can be injected into the prey's body. Beneath these two large fangs, there are **small teeth** in a row to assist their consumption of the prey，在兩個大型毒牙下方，可以看見成排的小牙齒，故答案為 **small teeth**。

- 第 **35** 題，觀看圖表並對應到 When you look at the part near the jaw, there is a **forked tongue** that lies between these teeth，在接近下顎，牙齒間有個分岔的舌頭，故答案為 **forked tongue**。

Test 1

Test 2

Test 3

Test 4

● 第 **36** 題，觀看圖表並對應到 The tongue can serve as a great tool to sense the prey nearby. And there is an expendable **glottis** that is behind the tongue. The function of the glottis is to help them make an air exchange while ingesting prey，關鍵字在舌頭後方，故答案為 **glottis**。

● 第 **37** 題，觀看圖表並對應到 Let's take a look at the nostril of the rattlesnake. The nostril and the tongue all assist the rattlesnake to sense olfactory stimuli. Near the nose, there is a heat sensing **pit**. Both the heat sensing pit and the eyes of the rattlesnake are able to sense radiation so that they get to find the prey and make a movement，關鍵字是在鼻子附近，故答案為 **pit**。

● 第 **38** 題，觀看圖表並對應到 Beneath it, there is a **venom duct** that transports the venom to larger fangs，故答案為 **venom duct**。

● 第 **39** 題，觀看圖表並對應到 The outer cover is the **fang sheath**，故答案為 **fang sheath**。

● 第 **40** 題，觀看圖表並對應到 What about the **venom gland**? It's an oval shape. Finally, we have to talk about the rattle. It is made up of hollow segments. Keratin makes these segments，故答案為 **venom gland**。

▶▶ 填空測驗

| Instruction | MP3 016

　　現在請再聽一次音檔，並做下列的測驗，檢視自己能否完成此填空測驗和強化自己聽力能力和拼字能力，降低並修正自己漏聽到聽力訊息的機會，大幅提升應考實力。

What seems to be a casual, agreeable afternoon in the **1.**_____ ____ can still contain many hazards concealed. In the forest, for an **2.**__ _____, maintaining a life for a few minutes can be considered a great achievement. What about in the case of squirrels? This is what we will be talking about during today's lecture.

In *Walden*, the author mentions the red squirrel, and it certainly is in the paradise, roaming freely on the **3.**_____ and running in such a haste. The red squirrel would arrive at the **4.**_____, reaching the corn to get the fitting ear. Sometimes with another new **5.**_____, and randomly toss away not yet finished **6.**_____ __. Then he would choose another corn, larger than himself, taking it back to the place where he lives. What a casual life? The **7.**_____ __ of the red squirrel certainly only gives us one of the **8.**_____ lives in the forest. A day like this is like a dream. Most of the time, most animals whether they are predators or preys do need to find the food, shelters, and most important of all, evade predators or confront with the predator.

So what about the life of the squirrel described by another author in *The Forest Unseen*. The depiction of the gray squirrel in a clumsy way. Instead of **9.**_____ on the leaf litter, it bumps its nose into the leaf litter.

By discussing these two books briefly, we are not yet mentioning something real and something danger. And we are about to... the danger is actually everywhere? What about those scenes that we frequently see in nature documentaries? An owl chasing down the squirrel, and with its **10.**_____ grasping the squirrel alive. Or the feisty squirrel mom, which demonstrates its **11.**_____ by confronting directly with the rattlesnake?

Or the cocky squirrel, which obviously bites off more than he can chew, and gets eaten by the cobra? Or the smart squirrel, which makes itself appear larger than normal so that the snake is **12.**_____ and then retreats. Or a group of squirrels circling around a few baby squirrels? Or a real fight-to-the-death scene between the squirrel and the king cobra. These are all **13.**_____ scenes that actually occur every moment.

The swiftness of the squirrels certainly makes them not that easily to be eaten and remain **14.**_____ under a few strikes of the king cobra. However, the king cobra does have something that is frightening, especially when they are larger. King cobras do possess a fatal **15.**_____ venom that can do a great deal of damage to the prey. So let's move on to the anatomy of the rattlesnake.

Rattlesnakes are known for their rattles at the end of the tails. Vibrations of the rattle will generate a loud **16.**_____ that can be served as a **18.**_____ to others. **17.**_____ snakes; however, are not afraid of this trick.

Let's take a look at the anatomy of the rattlesnakes. Their heads are comprised of many important parts that make them **19.**_____

There are two hollow, retractable fangs that can be clearly seen in the graph. Through these fangs, powerful venom can be **20.**_____ into the prey's body. Beneath these two large fangs, there are small **21.**_____ in a row to assist their consumption of the prey. When you look at the part near the jaw, there is a forked tongue that lies between these teeth.

The tongue can serve as a great tool to sense the prey nearby. And there is an expendable glottis that is behind the **22.**_____. The function of the glottis is to help them make an air exchange while **23.**_____ prey.

Let's take a look at the nostril of the rattlesnake. The **24.**_____ and the tongue all assist the rattlesnake to sense **25.**_____ stimuli. Near the nose, there is a heat sensing pit. Both the heat sensing pit and the eyes of the rattlesnake are able to sense **26.**_____ so that they get to find the prey and make a movement. Beneath it, there is a venom duct that **27.**_____ the venom to larger fangs. The outer cover is the fang sheath. What about the venom **28.**_____?

It's an oval shape. Finally, we have to talk about the rattle. It is made up of **29.**_____ segments. Keratin makes these segments. The noise that we hear is caused by the **30.**_____ of these segments...

參考答案

1. forest
2. insect
3. rooftop
4. field
5. ear
6. cobs
7. depiction
8. glimpse
9. swaggering
10. claws
11. bravery
12. dissuaded
13. authentic
14. unharmed
15. neurotoxic
16. noise
17. King
18. warning
19. fearsome
20. injected
21. teeth
22. tongue
23. ingesting
24. nostril
25. olfactory
26. radiation
27. transports
28. gland
29. hollow
30. vibrations

雅思聽力聖經 模擬試題 引用和出處

TEST 1 SECTION 3	"Misfortunes seldom come single." ***The History of Tom Jones, a Founding***
TEST 1 SECTION 4	"If my arm were to tire and that vicious beak came within striking distance." ***The Penguin Lessons***
TEST 2 SECTION 6	"I have therefore always thought it unreasonable in parents to desire to chuse for their children on this occasion." ***The History of Tom Jones, a Founding***
TEST 2 SECTION 6	"It is, however, true that, though a parent will not, I think, wisely prescribe, he ought to be consulted on this occasion; and in strictness, perhaps, should at least have a negative voice." ***The History of Tom Jones, a Founding***
TEST 2 SECTION 6	"The best marriages are when the parents choose for the girl." ***Gone with the Wind***
TEST 2 SECTION 6	"You shall do as you like." ***Middlemarch***
TEST 2 SECTION 6	"As pretending to be wise for young people- no uncle could pretend to judge what sort of marriage would turn out well for a young girl." ***Middlemarch***
TEST 2 SECTION 7	"I'm thirty-nine years old. I've got a wife that I can't get rid of. I've got varicose veins. I've got five false teeth." ***1984***
TEST 2 SECTION 7	"Yes, young people are usually blind to everything but their own wishes, and seldom imagine how much those wishes cost others." ***Middlemarch***
TEST 2 SECTION 7	"It's of no use, whatever I do, Mary, you are sure to marry Mr. Farebrother at last." ***Middlemarch***
TEST 2 SECTION 8	"How happy is he born and taught. That serveth not another's will." ***Middlemarch***

TEST 2 SECTION 8	"You've thrown away your education, and gone down a step in life, when I had given you the means of rising, that's all." ***Middlemarch***
TEST 2 SECTION 8	"I wash my hands for you, only hope, when you have a son of your own he will make a better return for the pains you spend on him." ***Middlemarch***
TEST 2 SECTION 8	"The career is built on carefully honed skills, ferocious work ethics, and good attitudes." ***Where You Go Is Not Who You Will Be***
TEST 3 SECTION 10	"To deny that beauty is an agreeable object to the eye, and even worthy some admiration, would be false and foolish." ***The History of Tom Jones, a Founding***
TEST 3 SECTION 10	"She had had her momentary flowering, a year perhaps, of wild-rose beauty and then she had suddenly swollen like a fertilized fruit and grown hard and red and coarse···" ***1984***
TEST 3 SECTION 10	"They are young in the ways of the world, and not yet open to the mortifying conviction that handsome young men must have something to live on as well as the plain." ***Pride and Prejudice***
TEST 4 SECTION 14	"Every profession, and every trade, required length of time, and what was worse, money; for matters are so constituted, that nothing out of nothing is not a truer maxim in physics than in politics." ***The History of Tom Jones, a Founding***
TEST 4 SECTION 15	"The whole of what Elizabeth had already heard, his claims on Mr. Darcy, and all that he had suffered from him, was now openly acknowledged and publicly canvassed." ***Pride and Prejudice***
TEST 4 SECTION 15	"We would like to here; therefore, locking doors for those who seem aloof to us. Vanity is an evil trait that makes invisible to facts presenting in front of our eyes." ***Pride and Prejudice***

Appendix
附錄　參考答案

Test 1
Listening 1 (1-40)

1. water
2. watermelon
3. muscle tissues
4. ostrich
5. protein
6. mango cactus
7. intestine
8. blood
9. chameleon
10. 890
11. I
12. B
13. C
14. G
15. J
16. A
17. H
18. F
19. D
20. E
21. B
22. D
23. C
24. I
25. G
26. B
27. C
28. A
29. C
30. B
31. oil slick
32. camouflage
33. plumage
34. waterproof
35. bill
36. webbed feet
37. the egg
38. flipper
39. the tail
40. gland

Test 2
Listening 2 (1-40)

1. sandstorms
2. insects
3. shelter
4. rattlesnake
5. thunderstorm
6. underpass
7. tunnel
8. flashlight
9. smartphone
10. scented candle
11. consulted
12. bystanders
13. market value
14. taboo
15. oil paintings
16. personality
17. liberal
18. guidance
19. refreshing
20. fiasco
21. pureness
22. protagonist
23. attention
24. desired
25. physical desire
26. prospect
27. vexing
28. envoy
29. satirizing
30. spontaneity
31. A
32. B
33. C
34. G
35. F
36. E
37. D
38. C
39. E
40. E

Test 3
Listening 3 (1-40)

1. caterpillars
2. music
3. scream
4. killer bee
5. old telephone
6. purple
7. dizziness
8. refrigerator
9. insecticide
10. closet
11. E
12. F
13. G
14. F
15. D
16. F
17. C
18. F
19. F
20. A
21. H
22. B
23. E
24. D
25. C
26. J
27. F
28. I
29. K
30. H
31. N
32. F
33. B
34. E
35. M
36. A
37. A
38. A
39. C
40. G

Test 4
Listening 4 (1-40)

1. remote control
2. poor eyesight
3. docile
4. toolbox
5. visual perception
6. fragrance
7. extinguisher
8. migraine
9. coffee mugs
10. elephant plate
11. I
12. E
13. B
14. C
15. D
16. F
17. I
18. C
19. G
20. A

21. F
22. B
23. E
24. G
25. A
26. C
27. F
28. D
29. E
30. B
31. ear
32. swagger
33. fangs
34. small teeth
35. forked tongue
36. glottis
37. pit
38. venom duct
39. fang sheath
40. venom gland

國家圖書館出版品預行編目(CIP)資料

雅思聽力聖經：模擬試題/韋爾著. -- 初版. --
新北市：倍斯特出版事業有限公司, 民111.
09 面； 公分. -- (考用英語系列；040)
ISBN 978-626-95434-9-6(平裝)
1.CST: 國際英語語文測試系統
2.CST: 考試指南

805.189　　　　　　　　　　111014045

考用英語系列 040

雅思聽力聖經－模擬試題（英式發音 附QR code音檔）

初　　刷　2022年9月
定　　價　新台幣550元

作　　者　韋爾
出　　版　倍斯特出版事業有限公司
發 行 人　周瑞德
電　　話　886-2-8245-6905
傳　　真　886-2-2245-6398
地　　址　23558 新北市中和區立業路83巷7號4樓
E - m a i l　best.books.service@gmail.com
官　　網　www.bestbookstw.com
總 編 輯　齊心瑀
特約編輯　郭玥慧
封面構成　高鍾琪
內頁構成　菩薩蠻數位文化有限公司
印　　製　大亞彩色印刷製版股份有限公司

港澳地區總經銷　泛華發行代理有限公司
地　　址　香港新界將軍澳工業邨駿昌街7號2樓
電　　話　852-2798-2323
傳　　真　852-3181-3973